Gift of John Fletcher
MCMXCV

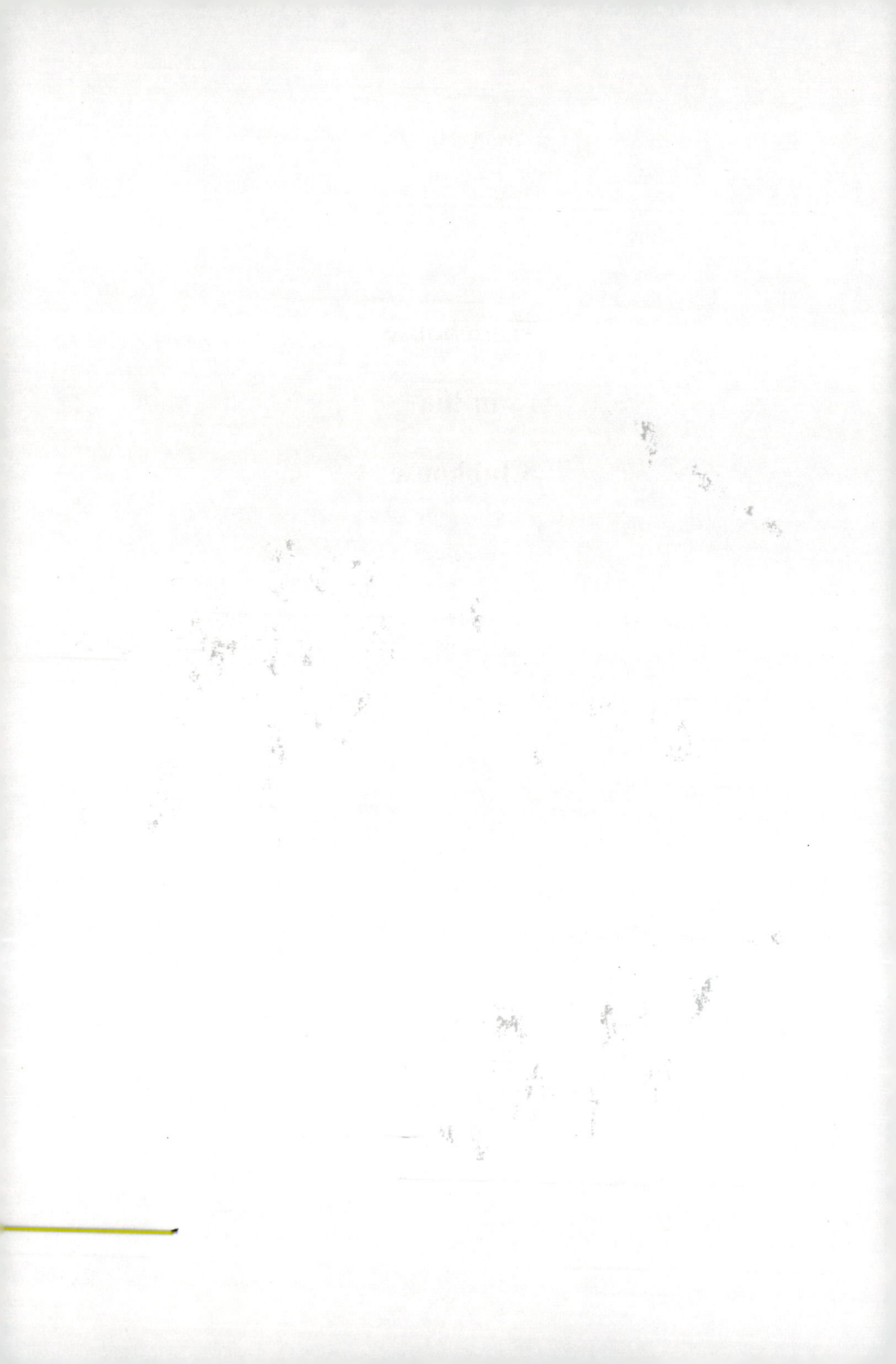

Wodehouse

in the

Clubhouse

Joseph Stocker's allergy

WODEHOUSE

IN THE

CLUBHOUSE

by

TONY RING

and

GEOFFREY JAGGARD

Illustrated by
Bernard Canavan

PORPOISE BOOKS

© Tony Ring and Geoffrey Jaggard 1994
Preface © Vallia Turner
who assert their rights as authors

Cover by Bernard Canavan
Illustrations © Porpoise Books
Quotations from P G Wodehouse
are reprinted by permission of A P Watt Limited
on behalf of the Trustees of the Wodehouse Estate
All rights reserved

Typesetting by Judith Cook, Maidenhead
Printed by Antony Rowe Limited, Chippenham, England

A CIP catalogue record for this book
is available from the British Library

Porpoise Books
68 Altwood Road
Maidenhead SL6 4PZ
ISBN 1 870303 14 4

GEOFFREY JAGGARD

by his daughter

Writer, author, broadcaster, journalist, with printers' ink coursing through his veins, fascinated by people, living by his voice and by his pen, this was Geoffrey William Jaggard, the complete communicator. A profound reader, collector and reviewer of books with that gifted memory which can pluck the exact literary quote to illustrate any given point.

His father, William Jaggard, was a Warwickshire man, born in Leamington Spa, who moved to Liverpool where he dealt in antiquarian books, maps, prints and philately. He married and returned with his young family to his native Warwickshire to live in Stratford–upon–Avon. He opened a shop in Sheep Street and called it "The Shakespeare Press". Here William Jaggard compiled and published a concordance to Shakespeare, the inspiration for the similar Wooster and Blandings volumes of his son.

The family link with Shakespeare is strong. In 1602 his ancestor, William Jaggard, was able to purchase outright a large printing and publishing house with which he had been associated for some time. It was here that he printed works by Raleigh and Bacon, and was also appointed official printer to the City of London — but it is as printer of Shakespeare's First Folio that he is best known.

Geoffrey Jaggard with his brothers attended the same school as Shakespeare had done and quickly became immersed in the Shakespearean atmosphere which that little town exudes. As a 16–year–old he took tea with Marie Corelli, played walk–on parts at the Shakespeare Memorial Theatre with Martin Harvey and Frank Benson who encouraged him and showed him great kindness, and who later gave his fiancée a little silver pig which he kept in his dressing room to bring him luck. He later took part in six of the Shakespeare Festivals.

It was around Stratford and the Cotswolds, roaming the lanes and meadows, that he developed his knowledge and great love of the countryside and especially its moths and butterflies. Later, joining the Liverpool Daily Post and Echo for 14 years as leader writer, book reviewer and drama critic, he greatly valued his visits back to Stratford for the quiet and tranquillity. Nevertheless, he could enthuse about the hustle and bustle of the big city, the boom of foghorns, the noise of the Mersey traffic, the clatter of clogs on cobbled streets, and the rattle of the printing presses, and later he found Elizabethan London with its pubs, alleys and dock area steeped in history greatly exciting.

When war seemed inevitable, and now with a wife and two children, he moved to Salisbury in Wiltshire to join Southern Command as Press Relations Officer, a non–combatant to liaise with the army and press correspondents, to see that they had their information and pictures but did not get in the way — at times, no mean task! Always writing, one achievement here was the writing of a daily broadsheet as field newspaper during the big exercises in preparation for D–Day. Following on into France and Germany, he was permanently affected by the horror of the concentration camps, and the sights of the gas chambers, seen and reported on for the first time; and it was not long after that that he was received into the Catholic Church.

Geoffrey Jaggard's great interests were in early keyboard music, Tudor style embroidery at which he was most accomplished, heraldry, natural history, literature, religion and history and it is interesting to note that these subjects occupied much of the printing time of that earlier William Jaggard.

Now we come to Bertie Wooster and to Blandings. In his later years, in his retirement enforced by ill–health, Geoffrey Jaggard returned to the books he had loved for so long, dusty, laid aside, but not forgotten. As we his children had left home we missed most of this; but I remember there was such excitement when a letter arrived from America — "I've just had another letter from Plum" he would say.

He said when he was compiling his Wodehouse companion volumes that it was like his father compiling the Shakespeare concordance: "The house revolved round slips of paper".

He tried to spread the pleasure that he enjoyed, and in *Blandings the Blest* wrote (p. 164) "It is when one has the dubious pleasure of taking apart a Wodehouse story for broadcasting purposes that one comes fully to appreciate the patience and skill of the plot construction". With his great interest in history, it is likely that he would have drawn up a coat of arms, at least for Lord Emsworth, but as yet it has not come to light. He would be delighted to see this fulfilment of his Wodehouse work at last.

This then was Geoffrey William Jaggard to whose widow P.G. — The Master — wrote "Although we had never met, I always looked upon him as a friend".

Vallia Turner, née Jaggard

THE MILLENNIUM WODEHOUSE CONCORDANCE

GENERAL INTRODUCTION

I was four years old when in 1952 Geoffrey Jaggard decided to prepare a concordance to Blandings, a decision immediately overridden by "an irrational desire to cover the whole opus embracing 80 books then completed". His text grew slowly for a number of reasons — he had a living to make, he had other interests, and by the time he had completed his survey of those eighty books another five had been published, and later, another four. But by the mid-1960s he was in a position to trawl his 350,000 word manuscript around a number of potential publishers, who unanimously thought it too long.

He then had a slice of luck — the BBC ran successive television series featuring the Jeeves and Wooster and the Blandings stories, and Macdonalds decided that the publication of *Wooster's World* and *Blandings the Blest* represented worthwhile gambles. Although Jaggard never met P G Wodehouse, he had his support for the project. In his introduction to *Wooster's World* he wrote:

> ....when [the Master] heard as long ago as 1952 what I was about, he not only bore the blow with fortitude but was kind enough to write both then and through the ensuing years, with the most heartening encouragement....

Alas, Geoffrey Jaggard died in 1970, before he was able to bring to publication any further sections of his work. The manuscript was subsequently sold at auction, and lay quietly until a chance conversation with a London book dealer in the summer of 1991 led to my acquiring it for my Wodehouse collection.

It was evident that the whole manuscript could still form a substantial foundation on which Jaggard's dream of a comprehensive concordance could be built. The most difficult questions to be faced were what to include and exclude, how to split the project into bite—size chunks, and how to remain faithful to the most important of Jaggard's objectives, which he expressed in the following terms:

*The main principle is to attract the reader by piquancy
and intriguing allusion back to the works themselves.*

The question of what to include has been solved on the principle that
the content should include all Wodehouse's published works except
autobiographical material, essays, journalistic articles, poems, lyrics
and plays. Exceptions are inevitably found — for example some of the
published plays which are closely based on novels, or formed the basis
for novels, are being included. Jaggard had restricted his review to UK
editions, whereas in many US editions the settings or names of the
characters might be different. It was also decided to review as many
original printings in magazines as possible to see whether differences
in the magazine and book versions might interest readers. And finally,
a surprising number of stories exist which can provide fascinating
material for the concordance but which have never been published in
book form. Jaggard did not concern himself with these, but as many
of the stories which fall into this category relate to characters who
appeared elsewhere, it was essential that they be included.

To try to facilitate the reader's task, whilst meeting Jaggard's objective,
the initial plan for the concordance has been to split it into eight
volumes, each of the first six based around — but not exclusively on
— major characters or narrators, while the final two volumes will cover
the remainder of the works in a more or less logical manner. Because
one of the things which endears readers to Wodehouse is his ability to
make his secondary characters interact with different major characters,
some members of his cast will appear in two or possibly three of the
volumes, but the comments to be found in each will differ.

A more extensive cross-referencing system than that used in
Jaggard's two books has been developed for this extended work — as
described from page xi. Each volume will contain a summary of novels
and short stories which it covers, and each will be assigned a
reference which will enable readers to identify not only the collection
of stories to which a comment refers but also the story itself. For the
benefit of readers who wish to trace the magazine entries, the
summary also lists magazine appearances.

TONY RING
August 1994

THE MILLENIUM WODEHOUSE CONCORDANCE

HOW TO USE THE REFERENCE SYSTEM

If the fancy of readers is tickled by the different references, allusions and comments in this work, it is hoped that they will be encouraged to read, or reread, the stories to which they refer. So the source of a character, place, quotation or other reference has been identified as specifically as necessary.

Most Wodehouse stories, particularly before the second world war, appeared in magazines in the US and the UK, as well as in book form in both countries. On occasion the book versions differed in a subtle, or even substantial, manner; differences could also be found between them and the magazines. Whilst occasionally such changes would be important to the story, more often they were editorial omissions for space reasons or minor changes in the name of a character or location. So difficult to trace are the magazines that by no means all have been reviewed and we would be pleased to hear from eagle-eyed readers who may be aware of additional items which could be included in any future revision.

In providing references, the principal source has been the first UK book publication. Where a change has been made in a later edition of which we are aware, or a story included in an omnibus edition for the first time, that is made clear. Entries unique to US books (again principally to the first editions) and to magazines have different references even where the story itself appears in the UK book.

Each short story or full length novel has been assigned a reference of three letters, as have collections of stories. Where the title of the story changes depending on where it appeared, it will have more than one reference, but only the UK book version will be used if the allusion can be found there. If reference is needed to a US collection of stories with the same name and relevant contents as a UK collection, at least as far as the golf stories are concerned, the 3 letter reference to the collection may be preceded by "US"; otherwise the collection will have a different reference. A reference to a magazine will be given in full or abbreviated as shown below. Each volume of the concordance concentrates on a group of linked stories, but inevitably some material from different stories will demand to be included. The table below, while concentrating on the comprehensive references, also identifies those imposters.

UK BOOK COLLECTIONS

CCU	The Clicking of Cuthbert	Herbert Jenkins	1922
FQO	A Few Quick Ones	Herbert Jenkins	1959
HOG	The Heart of a Goof	Herbert Jenkins	1926
LEO	Lord Emsworth & Others	Herbert Jenkins	1937
MLF	The Man With Two Left Feet	Methuen	1917
MMS	Mr Mulliner Speaking	Herbert Jenkins	1929
NSE	Nothing Serious	Herbert Jenkins	1950
PLP	Plum Pie	Herbert Jenkins	1966
TMU	The Man Upstairs	Methuen	1914

US BOOK COLLECTIONS

CRW	The Crime Wave at Blandings	Doubleday Doran	1937
DIV	Divots	George H Doran	1927
EGB	Eggs, Beans and Crumpets	Doubleday Doran	1940
GWT	Golf Without Tears	George H Doran	1924
TUW	The Uncollected Wodehouse	Seabury	1976
USFQO	A Few Quick Ones	Simon & Schuster	1959
USMMS	Mr Mulliner Speaking	Doubleday Doran	1930
USNSE	Nothing Serious	Doubleday	1951
USPLP	Plum Pie	Simon & Schuster	1967
YSP	Young Men in Spats	Doubleday Doran	1936

OTHER BOOK REFERENCES

ADD	A Damsel in Distress	Herbert Jenkins	1919
DOS	Doctor Sally	Methuen	1932
GOO	Good Morning, Bill (play)	Methuen	1928
HOW	Hot Water	Herbert Jenkins	1932
VGJ–JKC	Very Good, Jeeves (Jeeves and the Kid Clementina)	Herbert Jenkins	1930

REFERENCES FOR MAGAZINE TITLES

Argosy	Argosy (UK magazine)
ChicTrib	Chicago Tribune
Colliers	Colliers
Cosmo	Cosmopolitan
Elk	Elk's
ISM	Illustrated Sunday Magazine
John Bull	John Bull
McClure	McClure
NHM	National Home Monthly
Red	Red
SatEvePost	Saturday Evening Post
SLGD	St Louis Globe Democrat
Strand	Strand
ThisWeek	This Week
USArg	Argosy (US magazine)
Vanfair	Vanity Fair

MAGAZINE STORIES WITH REFERENCES QUOTED IN THE TEXT

Argosy–BSH	Argosy	The Battle of Squashy Hollow
Colliers–OBG	Colliers	Ordeal by Golf
Cosmo–IGY	Cosmopolitan	I'll Give You Some Advice
JohnBull–KYT	John Bull	Keep Your Temper, Walter
McClure–AMT	McClure	A Mixed Threesome
McClure–SGM	McClure	The Salvation of George Mackintosh
McClure–SUH	McClure	Sundered Hearts
Red–RPC	Red	Rollo Podmarsh Comes To
SatEvePost–BSH	Saturday Evening Post	The Battle of Squashy Hollow
SatEvePost–CFO	Saturday Evening Post	Chester Forgets Himself
SatEvePost–PRS	Saturday Evening Post	The Purification of Rodney Spelvin
Strand–HEA	Strand	The Heel of Achilles
Strand–TFT	Strand	Tee For Two
VanFair–TEH	Vanity Fair	The Eighteenth Hole

SHORT STORIES COVERED BY THIS VOLUME

UK Book reference	US Book reference	Magazine reference	Story reference	Story Title	Date
CCU	GWT	Strand McClure	AMT	A Mixed Threesome	3/21 6/20
CCU	GWT	 Strand Elk	COC UCC CUC	The Clicking of Cuthbert The Unexpected Clicking of Cuthbert Cuthbert Unexpectedly Clicks	 10/21 7/22
CCU	GWT	Strand McClure	COG	The Coming of Gowf	5/21 7/21
CCU	GWT	Strand SLGD ChicTrib	HEA	The Heel of Achilles	11/21 11–6/22 11–6/22
CCU	GWT	Strand McClure	LOH	The Long Hole	8/21 3/22
CCU	GWT	Colliers Strand	OBG KHC	Ordeal By Golf A Kink in his Character	6–12/19 2/20
CCU	GWT	Strand ChicTrib	ROS	The Rough Stuff	4/21 10–10/20
CCU	GWT	Strand McClure	SGM	The Salvation of George MacKintosh	6/21 9/21
CCU	GWT	Strand McClure	SUH	Sundered Hearts	12/20 12/20
CCU	GWT	Strand SatEvePost	WOW	A Woman is Only a Woman	10/19 7–6/19
FQO	USFQO	ThisWeek JohnBull	JBW KYT	Joy Bells for Walter Keep Your Temper, Walter	10–7/56 16–2/57
FQO	USFQO/ EGB	 Strand SatEvePost	SCM TFT	Scratch Man Tee for Two	 9/40 20–1/40
HOG	DIV	Strand Red	ARP RPC	The Awakening of Rollo Podmarsh Rollo Podmarsh Comes To	1/23 3/23
HOG	DIV	Strand SatEvePost	CFO	Chester Forgets Himself	5/24 7–7/23
HOG	DIV	Strand SatEvePost	HST	High Stakes	10/25 19–9/25
HOG	DIV	Strand SatEvePost	JGO	Jane Gets Off the Fairway	11/24 25–10/24

UK Book reference	US Book reference	Magazine reference	Story reference	Story Title	Date
HOG	DIV	Strand Liberty	KIW	Keeping In With Vosper	3/26 13–3/26
HOG	DIV	Strand Red	MPF PFO	The Magic Plus Fours Plus Fours	12/22 1/23
HOG	DIV	Strand SatEvePost	PRS	The Purification of Rodney Spelvin	9/25 22–8/25
HOG	DIV	Strand SatEvePost	RFQ	Rodney Fails to Qualify	3/24 23–2/24
HOG	DIV	Strand Red	THG	The Heart of a Goof	4/24 9/23
LEO	YSP	Strand Red	ALG OOD	There's Always Golf Not Out of Distance	3/36 4/36
LEO	YSP	Strand ThisWeek	FTL	Farewell to Legs	5/36 14–7/35
LEO	YSP	Strand Red	LEL ATT	The Letter of the Law A Triple Threat Man	4/36 2/36
MLF	—	Strand ISM	WIH WIV	Wilton's Holiday Wilton's Vacation	7/15 19–3/16
MMS	USMMS	Strand Liberty	PTT	Those in Peril on the Tee	5/29 21–5/27
NSE	USNSE	 Argosy	EXC HHB	Excelsior Hazards of Horace Bewstridge	 1–7/48
NSE	USNSE	 ThisWeek	FOC SBR	Feet of Clay A Slightly Broken Romance	 18–6/50
NSE	USNSE	 NHM	RHR RUR	Rodney Has a Relapse Rupert Has a Relapse	 2/49
NSE	USNSE	 Cosmo	TAH IGY	Tangled Hearts I'll Give You Some Advice	 9/48
NSE	USNSE		UFD	Up From the Depths	
PLP	USPLP	 SatEvePost Argosy	SLT BSH	Sleepy Time The Battle of Squashy Hollow	 5–6/65 10/65
TMU	—	Colliers	ARB	Archibald's Benefit	19–3/10
—	—	VanFair	TEH	The Eighteenth Hole	8/15

OTHER BOOKS COVERED BY THIS VOLUME

UK Book reference	US Book reference	Magazine reference	Story reference	Story Title	Date
DOS				Doctor Sally	
	CRW	Colliers	MEG	The Medicine Girl	4–7 to 1–8/31
GOO				Good Morning, Bill	

Note: CRW–MEG is the US publication of DOS, in turn a novel written from the play, GOO.

WODEHOUSE IN THE CLUBHOUSE

According to the Oldest Member, GOLF is a medicine for the soul, a corrective for sinful pride, which teaches human beings that whatever petty triumphs they may have achieved in other walks of life, they are merely human.

But according to tennis players, it is no more than 'cow–pasture pool'.

ABERCROMBIE: see **Fitch.**

ADDAMS, Charles: when in the throes of a hangover, would look like **Prof Farmer** clicking a sympathetic tongue. **(PLP–HST)**

AIKEN: South Carolina course where P G Wodehouse won his only golf trophy, a striped umbrella, beating some of the fattest retired businessmen in America in the process. **(Introduction, Golf Omnibus)**

ALCAZAR: the restaurant where **Rodney Spelvin** and **Jane Bates** were overseen, apparently hobnobbing, by **William Bates**. **(HOG–PRS)**

ALFRED: Evangeline Fisher's pet Airedale, prone to frolic round golfers until receiving one on his right foreleg at the seventh. **(HOG–KIW)**

ALPHONSE: a poodle with the **Botts**, but not the glanders, though described as a flea–storage depot. **(NSE–EXC)**

A MIXED THREESOME: a story **(CCU–AMT)** which, when it appeared in *McClure's* in June 1920, was not narrated by the **Oldest Member**, although it obtained that status in its CCU and GWT appearances.

1

AMALGAMATED LEAGUE of WORKING PLUMBERS, President of: down one golden matchbox. **(CCU–COG)**

AMBITION: achievement of a great, causes a man to feel filleted, as with Gibbon on finishing the *Decline and Fall of the Roman Empire.* **(FQO–SCM)**

AMY: **Jack Wilton**'s Bunbury, invented to enable him to enjoy his holiday without having characters such as **Spencer Clay** swooping down on him, but she brought him temporary grief. **(MLF–WIH)**

ANCIENT MARINER: like **George Mackintosh**, equipped with an eye that was a combination of gimlet and searchlight; but whereas the Ancient Mariner merely stopped a wedding guest on his way to a wedding, George Mackintosh could have stopped the Cornish Riviera Express on its way to Penzance. **(CCU–SGM)**

ANGELA: character in *The Love That Scorches*, who is seized by the Arab chief, flung on his horse, seared by his breath. **(HOG–RFQ)**

ANGLERS' REST: pub of considerable fame where **Mr Mulliner** holds court. **(MMS–PTT)**

ANIMAL GRAB: requires more athleticism than golf. **(CCU–WOW)**

ANNE, Queen (1665–1714): inspiration, if not model, for the table in **Bradbury Fisher**'s Crystal Boudoir. **(HOG–KIW)**

ANTONY (83–30BC): with **Cleopatra**, set the standard challenged by **Rollo Podmarsh** for getting swiftly off the mark. **(HOG–ARP)**

ARBMISHEL and ARREEVADON: are first among the famous Britishers whom **Vladimir Brusiloff** is looking forward to meeting. **(CCU–COC)**

ARMOUR, Tommy: tells **Cyril Grooly** to keep his head down. **(PLP–SLT)**

ARTBASHIEKEFF: Felicia Blakeney's ideal would not know whether, was a suburb of Moscow or a new drink. (HOG–CFO)

ARTHUR, King: in whose sixth–century day nobody thought the worse of a young knight if he suspended all his social and business engagements in favour of a search for the Holy Grail. (CCU–SUH)

ASCOBARUCH: the sinister half–brother of King Merolchazzar. (CCU–COG)

ASTOR, Lady (1879–1964): indebted to **Jack Fosdyke** for the opportunity of making a quip to **Lord Beaverbrook**. (NSE–FOC)

ATTILA the HUN (406–453): might have broken off his engagement to **Agnes Flack**. See also **Genghis Khan**. (FQO–SCM; LEO–ALG)

AUBUSSON CARPETS: provided in Editors' offices for prospective contributors to knock their heads on, reverently. (CCU–COG)

AUCHTERMUCHTIE: home club of **Tammas McMickle**. (CCU–SUH)

AUDEN, Wystan Hugh (1907–1973): read by **Sidney McMurdo** to **Celia Todd**, and substituted for **Erle Stanley Gardner** by **Agnes Flack**. (NSE–TAH; Cosmo–IGY)

AVILION: an island valley brought to **Rodney Spelvin**'s mind by the vista on the fourth at **Mossy Hill**. Also the basis of **Archibald Mealing**'s one memorised piece of poetry, following his being discovered smoking many years earlier. (HOG–RFQ; MUP–ARB)

BABYLON: an inhabitant of ancient, would have beamed approvingly on the clubhouse erupting with roses, smilax, Chinese lanterns, gold-toothed saxophonists, giggling girls and light refreshments. (LEO–FTL)

BAER, Bugs: see **Edna St Vincent Millay**. (NSE–TAH)

Cuthbert Banks insisted on playing it where it lay

4

BAILEY, Rupert: a crony of the **Oldest Member**, acts as his fellow–judge in the golf match over the longest hole in the world. (**CCU–LHO**)

BALBOA, Vasco Núñes de (1475–1517): disinherited by stout **Cortez** and the equally stout **Cortes**. (**CCU foreword; CCU–SUH**)

BANKS, Abe Mitchell Ribbed–faced Mashie: the firstborn of **Cuthbert Banks** is almost baptised as. (**CCU–COC**)

BANKS, J Cuthbert (Cootaboot): ...resident of **Wood Hills** who after nearly incapacitating **Raymond Parsloe Devine** firmly insisted on standing on the table and playing his ball with a niblick where it lay. A modest and likeable young man who, though proficient enough a golfer to win the French Open Championship, play with Abe Mitchell often and be partnered with **Harry Vardon**, admits diffidently the truth of the charge preferred by **Adeline Smethurst**, the girl he loves, to wit, that he is sadly lacking in culture, and joins the local Literary Society forthwith. After attending eleven debates and fourteen lectures on such subjects as *vers libre* poetry and the Neo–Scandinavian Movement in Portuguese Literature, grows so enfeebled that he has to take a full iron for his mashie shots. Relief arrives in the unlikely form of the Angry Young Russian novelist **Brusiloff**.

> "Banks!" cried Brusiloff. "Not Cootaboot Banks?"
>
> "Well, it's Cuthbert."
>
> "Yais! Yais! Cootaboot!" There was a rush and a swirl as the effervescent Muscovite burst his way through the throng, then, stooping swiftly, kissed him on both cheeks before Cuthbert could get his guard up. "I saw you win ze French Open. Great! Great! Grand! Superb! Hot stuff and you can say I said so! Will you permit one who is but eighteen at **Nijni Novgorod** to salute you once more?"

(**CCU–COC**)

BANNISTER, William: of **Woollam Chersey Manor House,** Hants. See **William Paradene.** (DOS, GMB)

BAPTIST CHURCH: the **Oldest Member**'s resignation from which was the only alternative to giving up playing with **Alexander Paterson.** (CCU–OBG)

BARRI, du: to whom **Bradbury Fisher**'s bedroom at **Goldenville** is attributed. (HOG–KIW)

BARTLETT: his *Familiar Quotations* assisted **Archibald Mealing.** (MUP–ARB)

BASSETT, Alexander: main stem of the grapevine in the **Oldest Member**'s golf club. (LEO–ALG)

BATES, Anastasia: one of those small, roseleaf girls to whom good men instinctively want to give a stroke a hole, even though she reached the Semi–final of the Ladies' Open, and on whom bad men automatically prey; is a younger sister of the phlegmatic **William.** Despite the awful warning provided by her sister–in–law's rapprochement with the roué **Rodney Spelvin,** she falls for that libertine in a big way.

> "If", she said, "he beckoned to me in the middle of
> a medal round, I would come. . . ."

One result of their match is the appearance of **Timothy Bobbin** and some inspired poetry from the school of Milne.

(HOG–PRS; NOS–RHR)

BATES, Braid Vardon: inevitably the firstborn of that notable golfing pair, **William Bates** and **Jane Packard,** forced to inhabit a cupboard during their sojourn in the artistic quarter. Being untrained, he holds his mashie all wrong, causing Jane to realise how much she had neglected her duty as a mother. A vocal child, for which William's remedy involves the judicious use of green baize cloths. Receives intensive instruction from a leading pro for the Children's Cup.

Probably the rudest child this (but which?) side of the Atlantic Ocean, not afraid openly to blackmail his parents. **(HOG–JGO; NSE–RHR)**

BATES, Grace: one of three girls loved by one man, thereby helping him to be worth his salt. **(MLF–WIH)**

BATES, Jane: a loving mother, but prepared to push her chickabiddy's nose sideways. **(NSE–RHR)**

BATES, William: not in the Petruchio class of wooer, in affairs of the heart he moves with caution. There was however an understanding that, if both continued to survive and were eligible to wed, and if he could somehow be stimulated, or activated, into the act of proposing marriage, **Jane Packard**, *mutatis mutandis*, other things being equal, *pari passu*, and *ad rem*, would on certain conditions and without prejudice, consider seriously whether to accept him or not, and the more observant reader of these pages will already have deduced the outcome. A somewhat ruminant, ox–like, bovine, almost lymphatic — one might even say placid — sort of man. Held three things in the smallest esteem — slugs, poets and caddies with hiccups. **(HOG–RFQ, JGO, PRS; NSE–RHR)**

BAYSIDE: passed in silence after the **Oldest Member**'s singing was compared to farmyard imitations by **Arthur Jukes**. **(CCU–LOH)**

BEATRICE: under **Dante**'s gaze. **(HOG–ARP)**

BEAVERBROOK, Lord (1879–1964): amused by **Lady Astor**. **(NSE–FOC)**

BELL–BOY, a: at the Superba, **Bingley–on–Sea**; recommended vinegar for hysterics, enjoyed watching lovers' tiffs involving the destruction of china, chairs and table–legs. **(DOS)**

BELUS: a god in front of whose altar a holy fire burns day and night. **(CCU–COG)**

7

BENNETT, Arnold (1867–1931): in an essay, warns young bachelors to proceed with a certain caution in matters of the heart.

> "They should, he asserts, first decide whether or not they are ready for love; then, whether it is better to marry earlier or later; thirdly, whether their ambitions are such that a wife will prove a hindrance to their career. These romantic preliminaries concluded, they may grab a girl and go to it."

Rollo Podmarsh scorned such advice. **(HOG–ARP)**

BESSEMER, Smallwood: a columnist for a morning paper and a confirmed adviser, described by **Celia Todd** as the sort of human fiend who ought to be eating peanuts in the front row at a bull fight. Became engaged to **Agnes Flack**, but realised he would only ever have that impersonal admiration which is inspired in one by anything large, like the Empire State Building or the Grand Canyon of Arizona. **(NSE–TAH)**

BEWSTRIDGE, Horace: the finest golfer and bravest wooer in the long experience of the **Oldest Member**, unhesitatingly spanks his loved one's favourite aunt together with an assortment of other relatives and pets when she interferes with his putting on the eighteenth green, to the eternal joy of **Vera Witherby**, the beloved, and **Sir George Copstone**, who thought it precisely what the woman needed. **(NSE–EXC)**

BILL: the caddie to **Mitchell Holmes**, who was expected to eat apples at the thirteenth hole of the match against **Alexander Paterson**. **(Colliers–OBG)**

BINGHAM, Ralph: plays a match on the longest hole in the world, with the whole world as the prize, but proves less adept as a golf–lawyer than he had anticipated. Renamed **Rollo** in **GWT–LOH**. **(CCU–LOH)**

BINGLEY, Marcella: a formidable, weather–beaten individual with bobbed hair and the wrists of a welterweight pugilist, who had once competed in the Open.

(Yes. The Ladies Open.) **(CCU–ROS)**

BINGLEY, Teddy: morose **Marois (or Marvis) Bay** golfer. **(MLF–WIH)**

BINGLEY–ON–SEA: golfer's **Mecca** on the south coast of England. **(DOS)**

BINSTEAD, Patricia: secretary to **Mr Popgood**, and fiancée of **Cyril Grooly**. **(PLP–SLT)**

BLACKWELL: see **CROSSE**.

BLACKWELL, Edward: whose standard **Bradbury Fisher** sought to emulate in the matter of giving the ball the nastiest bang it had ever had. **(HOG–HST)**

BLAKE, Rupert: the Vicar's partner when the Rev. smashed his putter on the last green, being unable to relieve his feelings in any other way. **(HOG–CFO)**

BLAKENEY, Crispin: an eminent young reviewer and essayist, studying conditions in India with a view to a series of lectures. At school with **Chester Meredith**, where he was despised as the world's worst and kicked seven hundred and forty–six times by Chester. To his sister **Felicia** he wouldn't do, and if he tries to set foot across the threshold of the married Merediths, **Joseph** will be given work to do. **(HOG–CFO)**

BLAKENEY, Felicia: a beautiful 23–year old, with a lissom figure and a perfect face; hair of deep chestnut, blue eyes and a nose small and laid back with about as much loft as a light iron. Daughter of **Wilmot Royce**, brother of **Crispin**, owner of the dog **Joseph**, and parsnip suppressor. To **Chester Meredith**, she is the alligator's Adam's apple. Impresses the cognoscenti with her swing, employing a nice, crisp, snappy half–slosh with a good full follow–through. **(HOG–CFO)**

BLIGH, Captain (c1753–1817) : of the Bounty, a realistic model for comparison with **Walter Judson** when on the links. **(FQO–JBW)**

BLIZZARD: Finest English butler on Long Island, N.Y., and reputedly the finest in the State, serving **Bradbury Fisher** prior to a transfer to **J Gladstone Bott**. Had previously been fifteen years in the service of an earl, and his appearance suggested that throughout those fifteen years he had not let a day pass without its pint of port. He radiated port and popeyed dignity. He had splay feet and three chins, and when he walked his curving waistcoat preceded him like the advance guard of some royal procession. **(HOG–HST)**

BLUEMANTLE PURSUIVANT at ARMS: lost his blue mantle. **(NSE–FOC)**

BOBBIN, Timothy: the subject of **Rodney Spelvin**'s biographical lapse into poetry, possibly not a Milne miles away from plagiarism. One example was rejected because it over–stressed the sex motif:

> Timothy Bobbin has a canary.
> About its sex opinions vary.
> If it just goes tweet–tweet,
> We shall call it Pete,
> But if it lays an egg, we shall switch to Mary.

(NSE–RHR)

BODGER, Colonel: a tottery performer of advanced years, martyr to lumbago for a decade, and selected by **Rollo Podmarsh** as his opponent in a real money match. **(HOG–ARP)**

BOOKSY WEEKLY: commissions an urgent article on *Albert Camus and the Aesthetic Tradition* from **Cosmo Botts**. **(FQO–JBW)**

Blizzard – the finest English butler on Long Island

BOOTLE, Duke of: at whose house–party **Mrs Bradbury Fisher** succumbs to temptation. **(HOG–HST)**

BOOTLE, Mr: an unknown basso asked if that was. **(HOG–PRS)**

BORGIAS: Italians of the Middle Ages dropping in to take pot–luck with, would have felt like **Rollo Podmarsh**. **(HOG–ARP)**

BORGUM (or BORGLUM), Gotzon (1867–1941): butcher of the South Dakota environment whose sculptures on the side of Mount Rushmore included the busts of just about everybody other than the Infant Samuel. **Agnes Flack** looked at **Smallwood Bessemer** as if she were something carved by. **(Cosmo – IGY)**.

BORSTAL, Dr: Sally Smith's substitute. **(DOS; GOO)**

BOTT, J Gladstone: fated to be the lifelong rival, in fame or notoriety, of **Bradbury Fisher**. The latter makes his first million first, but **JG**'s first divorce suit gets half–a–column and two sticks more publicity than **Fisher**'s. At **Sing Sing**, where each spent several happy years of early manhood, they ran neck and neck for the prizes which that institution has to offer. When his fifteen–foot putt to win is smitten off–line, hits a worm cast, bounds off to the left for a couple of yards, hits another, bounds to the right, hits a twig, leaps to the left and clatters into the tin, he describes it as "gauging the angles to a nicety". **(HOG–HST)**

BOTTS, Cosmo: a Civil Servant and book reviewer son of **Ponsford** and **Lavender** with a tendency to set everybody right about everything, causing strong men to hide behind trees. **(FQO–JBW)**

BOTTS, Horace: son of **Lavender** and **Philibert**, who acts as caddie to **Walter Jukes**. **(JohnBull–KYT)**

BOTTS, Irwin: schoolboy son of **Ponsford** and **Lavender**, is in love with **Dorothy Lamour** and not making much of a go of it. **(NSE–EXC)**

BOTTS, Lavender Bingley: wife of **Ponsford** and **Philibert,** mother of **Cosmo, Horace** and **Irwin,** and aunt of both **Vera Witherby** and **Angela Pirbright,** has a private telephone to fairyland. Like all women with three names, she wrote books — but with titles that include *My Chums The Pixies, Many of My Best Friends are Mosquitoes,* and *Many of My Best Friends are Fieldmice.* Unable to decide whether to call her forthcoming book *Elves on the Golf Course* or *Elves in the Sunshine.* **(NSE–EXC; FQO–JBW; JohnBull–KYT)**

BOTTS, Ponsford (or Philibert): extrovert husband of **Lavender** and uncle of **Vera Witherby,** is given to relating stories about Irishmen, accompanied by prods in the ribs, but cannot tell a Scottish dialect story dealing with hiccups without getting a nosebleed. **(NSE–EXC; FQO–JBW; JohnBull–KYT)**

BOULE: one of **Bradbury Fisher**'s tables, not a French game. **(HOG–KIW)**

BOWLS: ranked by the **Oldest Member** with the juvenile pastime of marbles. **(HOG–ARP)**

BOYD, Millicent: on hearing **Mitchell Holmes**'s masterly impression of a Pekingese having a difference of opinion with a bulldog, realises that she can never feel quite the same about other men. **(CCU–OBG)**

BOY SCOUT POCKET KNIFE: useful weapon for dealing with sharks in the Indian Ocean. **(NSE–FOC)**

BRACKETT, Evangeline: though practising diligently for the Ladies' Spring Medal at her golf club, doubles her handicap by falling for the meretricious charms of **Legs Mortimer.** Did not say 'Tee-hee' when topping a drive, which enabled her to retain some humanity. **(LEO–FTL)**

BRAID, James (1870–1950): spoke sadly of those who sin against their better selves by stiffening their muscles and heaving. **Mortimer Sturgis** would have chosen his birthplace as an ideal honeymoon spot. A non–dancer, but author of *Golf Without Tears, Braid on Taking Turf, Braid on the Push–Shot, On the Pivot* and *Advanced Golf.* (HOG–THG,PRS; CCU–WOW,AMT,SGM,ROS; DOS; GOO)

BRAY, Eunice: a girl golfer whose ravishing beauty is matched only by her pronounced hauteur until she meets the timid and diffident **Ramsden Waters**. A year or so later, as wife and mother, she mystifies hearers by the remark "Chicketty wicketty wicketty wipsy pop!" (CCU–ROS)

BRAY, Wilberforce: small, obese brother of **Eunice**, whose alluring trouser–seat (Wilberforce's, not Eunice's) a stronger man than **Ramsden Waters** would have found difficult to resist when informed that he had missed the ball. See **Gabriel, Archangel**. (CCU–ROS)

BREAM, Wilberforce: like the poltroon **Alfred Jukes**, is a paltry and regrettable golfer who, though playing from scratch, has been known to concede a hole for the frivolous reason that he has sliced his ball into a hornet's nest and is reluctant to play it where it lay. Capable of giving **Ernest Plinlimmon** ten and beating him only if he has not been turned down by **Clarice Fitch**. (NSE–EXC; LEO–ALG)

BRENTANO: the New York emporium and prospective supplier of the whole of **Cora Spottsworth**'s output. (NSE–FOC)

BRIDLEY–IN–THE–WOLD: **Jack Wilton**'s home town, which to a man looks on him as a strong man who will support them. (MLF–WIH)

BRINKLEY, Eustace: **George Mackintosh** can give a stroke a hole to the inferior, and trample on his corpse. (CCU–SGM)

BROSTER: beat **Perkins** on the eighteenth amongst a medley of shrill animal cries. (HOG–HST)

BROWN, Dr: sitting in a snug surgery surrounded by antidotes. (HOG–ARP)

Wilberforce Bream and the hornets' nest

Vladimir Brusiloff

16

BROWN, Montague: plays a freak game of golf against **Herbert Widgeon**. As a twenty–four, is entitled to shout 'Boo!' three times during the round at moments selected by himself. **(CCU–LOH)**

BROWN, Percival: takes up the **Oldest Member**'s wager of twelve golf balls on **Grace Forrester**'s intentions. **(CCU–WOW)**

BROWN, Reggie: one of the best sleuths in the service of the **Quick Results Agency.** **(HOG–PRS)**

BROWNING, Robert (1812–1889): the **Oldest Member** wondered whether it was wise for **Chester Meredith** to emulate a pretty, poetic idea in *Last Ride Together* by, in playing a last round with **Felicia Blakeney**. Taken without anaesthetic by **McCay**. **(HOG–CFO; MUP–ARB)**

BROWNLOW: sausage supplier to the **Bates**, the best **William** has ever bitten. **(HOG–JGO)**

BRUSILOFF, Vladimir: Angry Young Russian Novelist, specialising in grey studies of stark despair, wherein nothing happens till page 380, where the moujik decides to commit suicide. Wears a dense zareba of hair through which his eyes — with an expression not unlike that of a cat in a strange backyard surrounded by small boys — were visible. Concedes that, as novelists, **P G Wodehouse** and **Tolstoi** are not bad, even though not good, but spits him of all contemporary A. Y. R.s, and emphatically spits him of **Sovietski** and **Nastikoff**. **(CCU–COC)**

BUNG–HO: see **honk–honk**.

BUNTING, George: lost to **Sidney McMurdo** in the Club Championship. **(FQO–SCM)**

BURKE, Lottie: has no family. Claims to be **Mr Paradene**'s medicine, a viewpoint disputed by his doctor. A Balham Burke — there were Burkes in Balham before they built the first cinema. Married Bixby before he was ennobled, then **Edwin Higginbotham**. **(DOS; GOO)**

17

BURNS, Mr: one of the best players in the club, but seldom manages to reach eighty. **(HOG–ARP)**

BUTLER: routed by **Archibald Mealing** in the **Cape Pleasant** championship. **(MUP–ARB)**

BYNG, Wilmot: according to the **Sage**, an engaging young fellow with a drive almost as long as the **Pro's**, his one defect being impatience. He has drawn **Gwendoline Poskitt** as his partner for life's medal round, even though she considers him to be an obstinate, fat–headed son of an army mule. **(LEO–LEL)**

CAMBRIDGE: the varsity attended by the **Oldest Member**. **(CCU–HEA)**

CAMOMILE TEA: always given to the sick in the country. **(DOS; GOO)**

CAMPBELL, Mary: to the narrator, small and insignificant, with ordinary eyes and hair; but to **Jack Wilton** wonderful. Plays golf and tennis but is inscrutable, until stranded in a bay with the tide coming up. **(MLF–WIH)**

CAPE PLEASANT: New Jersey club whose members were easy–going refugees from other clubs, who pottered round the links. **(MUP–ARB)**

CAPULETS: and **Montagues**, dropping in on a reunion of, was like being in the same room as **Ralph Bingham** and **Arthur Jukes**. **(CCU–LOH)**

CARNEGIE HALL: where **Vladimir Brusiloff** lectured. **(GWT–COC)**

CARSTAIRS, Revell: drawn from **Sidney McMurdo** for *Furnace of Sin*. **(NSE–FOC)**

CASE, Mabel: chestnut hair, turned-up nose and a habit of flinging herself on **George Porter**'s neck and kissing him fondly. But is she wholly faithful? Why did she act in the same way with **George Prosser?** (FQO-JBW; John Bull-KYT)

CAT, a passing: Mortimer Gooch tripped over, on the eve of the semi-final of the **President's Cup.** Remarkably he, not the cat, scratched, thereby giving **Horace Bewstridge** a final place. (NSE-EXC)

CATHERINE II, Empress of Russia (1729-1796): like so many of the world's greatest women, would have been out of place at **Woollam Chersey.** (DOS; GOO)

CHARCOAL POISONING: Dwight Messmore's description of the cause of an indisposition following a teetotal evening, with nothing to drink but champagne, brandy, chartreuse, benedictine, curaçao, crème de menthe, kummel and whisky. (NSE-UFD)

CHARLES I, King (1600-1649): planted an oak at **Woollam Chersey.** (DOS)

CHAUCER, Geoffrey (c1345-1400): included in *The Squiere's Tale* the line:

Therefore behoveth him a ful long spoone

although, as was pointed out, with the later rubber-cored ball, an iron would achieve the same distance. (HOG-Preface)

CHESNEY, Wallace: has riches, perfect health and **Charlotte Dix** as a fiancée, he dances, rides, plays bridge and polo with equal skill, is the best-looking man for miles around, but is kept modest and unspoilt because of his rotten golf. (HOG-MPF)

CHESTERTON, Gilbert Keith (1874-1936): see **Flesho.**

CHEVALIER BAYARD: Angela Pirbright is assumed to be linking her lot with a. (FQO-JBW)

CHICKETTY-WICKETTY: etc, etc, see **Eunice Bray**. (CCU-ROS)

CHINA: the situation in which was the subject of discussion between **Pirbright** and **Agnes Flack**'s wolfhound. (NSE-TAH)

CLAUDE, little: may take 200 or 220 approach shots to reach the ninth green. (CCU-AMT)

CLAY, Spencer: when he got hold of anything, **Marois Bay** (or, as some say, **Marvis Bay**) got it hot and fresh a few hours later, for he was a slack-jawed youth constitutionally incapable of preserving a secret. Always had a dozen hard-luck stories in stock. (MLF-WIH)

CLEOPATRA (69-30BC): would have been less imperious if outed in the first round of the Ladies' Singles. Would have been out of place at **Woollam Chersey**. Recalled to mind by **Clarice Plinlimmon**. See **Antony**. (HOG-MPF, ARP; LEO-TAG; DOS; GOO)

COHAN, George: the only poet not classified as punk by **Archibald Mealing**. (MUP-ARB)

COHEN BROS: of the City of London, second-hand clothiers, presumably an offshoot of the menswear specialists in Covent Garden. They do not confine their trade to Gents' Wear, it being a museum of derelict goods of every description where you can get a second-hand revolver, a second-hand sword or a second-hand umbrella. Or do a cheap deal in field-glasses, trunks, dog collars, canes, photograph frames, attaché cases, or bowls for goldfishes. Or putters of lunatic design. Or plus fours of unusual tartan — see **Plus Fours**. (HOG-MPF)

COHEN, Irving: sells **Wallace Chesney** a fireman's helmet. (HOG-MPF)

COHEN, Isidore: sells **Wallace Chesney** a putter, a dog collar and a set of studs. (HOG-MPF)

COHEN, Lou: sells **Wallace Chesney** golfing breeches — see **Plus Fours.** (Had just sold a customer, who had only come for a cap, two pairs of trousers and a miniature aquarium for keeping newts in.) **(HOG–MPF)**

COLERIDGE, Samuel Taylor (1772–1834):

The true meaning of the words

Clothing the palpable and familiar
With golden exhalations of the dawn.

from Coleridge's play *The Death of Wallenstein*, Act 1, Scene 1, is made clear to the **Oldest Member.** **(CCU–LOH)**

COLOSSEUM, The: **Mortimer Sturgis** speculated whether **Abe Mitchell** would use a full brassey to carry it, and whether James Barnes would prefer a Brassy. **(CCU–SUH; McClure–SUH)**

CONSCIENCE, Voice of: the telephone going off like a bomb in **Jane Bates's** ear sounded like. **(HOG–PRS)**

CONSOLIDATED PEANUTS: the news that it had gone up 15 points and that **Mortimer Sturgis** had sold out at a hundred and eleven would not make **Betty Weston** feel the trembling of divine ecstasy. **(McClure's–AMT)**

COODEN BEACH: achieves fame when selected by the Committee of the Drones Club as the venue for the annual golf rally. **(NSE–BSB)**

COPSTONE, Sir George: a tall, thin, bony Englishman, one of the Sussex Copstones, left over from the 1860s. Found visiting America and residing with **Ponsford Botts.** Beat **Peter Willard** on the fifteenth, giving thirty-eight. Runs a vast system of chain stores in England. **(NSE–EXC)**

CORTES, Hernando ("Stout") (1485–1547): stared with eagle eyes at the Pacific, while his men occupied themselves in other ways. **(CCU–WOW)**

Mortimer Sturgis contemplates a hazard

CORTEZ: see **Cortes**

CRACKA–BITTA–ROCK: **Bradbury Fisher** and **Rupert Worple** belong to this fraternity at **Sing Sing**. (HOG–KIW)

CROCODILE: an animal which, when described by explorers to beautiful young girls, increases in length from thirty to fifty feet in one paragraph. (CCU–AMT)

CROQUET MALLET: identified by **Mortimer Sturgis** as the solution to putting problems. (CCU–AMT)

CROSSE: Who now can explain what it was about, that first attracted **Blackwell**? (CCU–WOW)

CRUMBLES, R P: a hard taskmaster who instructed **Horace Bewstridge** to throw his final against **Sir George Copstone**, but was unable to breach a chasm. (NSE–EXC)

The Marvis Bay Mug

24

CUPS

The cups, pewter mugs, medals and championships which were
fought for, won and lost, or dreamed about, were numerous.

All-Day Sucker	Competed for by children under seven	**(NSE-EXC)**
Amateur Championship	Dreamed about by Chester Meredith	**(HOG-CFO)**
American Amateur	Dreamed about by Chester Meredith	**(HOG-CFO)**
	Missed by Vincent Jopp by one hole	**(HOG-HEA)**
American Open	Dreamed about by Chester Meredith	**(HOG-CFO)**
Atlanta, Georgia	Infants' All-In Championship open to those of both sexes not yet having finished teething	**(HOG-HST)**
Cape Pleasant	Championship, won by Archibald Mealing	**(MUP-ARB)**
Children's Cup	For which Braid Bates has professional instruction	**(NSE-RHR)**
Club Championship	McMurdo v Pickering	**(FQO-SCM)**
East Bampton	Women's Singles	**(NSE-FOC)**
Grandmother's Umbrella	At the home course	**(NSE-EXC)**

July Medal	At the home course, Wallace Chesney and Raymond Gandle being favourites	(HOG–MPF)
Ladies' Open	Semi–final reached by Anastasia Bates	(HOG–PRS)
Ladies' Vase	Handicap event won twice in successive years by Agnes Flack	(NSE–TAH)
Little–Mudbury–in–the–Wold	Medal won by Amanda Trivett's fiancé	(CCU–LOH)
Marvis Bay	A great medal–play handicap tournament, the prize being a handsome pewter mug about the size of the old oaken bucket	(HOG–THG)
Mixed Foursomes		(LEO–ALG)
Mossy Heath	Annual Ladies' Invitation Tournament	(HOG–RFQ)
Open	Dreamed about by Chester Meredith	(HOG–CFO)
Outer Isles	Ladies' Open won by the Princess of the Outer Isles	(CCU–COG)
President's Cup	At the home course, won twice by Chester Meredith	(HOG–CFO)
President's Cup	For those with a handicap of eighteen or over	(FQO–JBW)

Rabbits' Umbrella	Open to those with a handicap over eighteen	**(NSE–RHR)**
Rockport Championship	Derrick outmanoeuvred by Maxwell, so wins	**(TEH)**
Squashy Heath Invitation Tournament		**(FQO–SCM)**
Squashy Hollow – UK	Invitation Tournament, attended by William Bates	**(HOG–RFQ)**
Squashy Hollow – US	Golf Club Invitation Tournament, sixth sixteen, for a small pewter cup value three dollars, won by Bradbury Fisher	**(HOG–KIW)**
Summer Medal	Interrupted by a sheep	**(LEO–ALG)**
Weekly Medal	At the home course, for the lowest net at a weekly handicap	**(CCU–AMT)**
Wissahicky Glen	Vincent Jopp won five successive monthly medals	**(CCU–HEA)**

DAMON: see **Pythias**.

DANTE Alighieri (1265–1321): might have gazed at **Beatrice** on a particularly sentimental morning as **Rollo** gazed at **Mary**. (**HOG–ARP**)

D'ARTAGNAN: of the links, **Joe Poskitt**. (**LEO–LEL**)

DAVID: see **Jonathan**.

DELAMERE, Claud: a character in chapter 32 of *The Man of Chilled Steel*, where he drags **Lady Matilda** around the smoking–room by her hair because she gave the rose from her bouquet to the Italian count. (**CCU–ROS**)

DELANCEY, Cyril: a star detective. (**HOG–PRS**)

DELL, Ethel M: **Jane Bates** reflects that after all **Rodney Spelvin** is not an Ethel M Dell heavyweight libertine, but only a welterweight egg of evil. (**HOG–PRS**)

DENMARK, King of: Men from Missouri might suggest one tells it to. (**MUP–ARB**)

DENTON, Eddie: a fearless hunter given to enthralling young ladies with stories of his jungle adventures among the **Ongos**. Despite being **Mortimer Sturgis**'s best friend, he traps **Betty Weston** and prises her away from **Mortimer**'s grasp. (**CCU–AMT**)

DEPUTY MASTER OF THE ROYAL BUCKHOUNDS: one of the positions of trust held by **Jack Fosdyke**. (**NSE–FOC**)

DERRICK, B Rockleigh: with traits and a daughter remarkably similar to his evident relation Professor Patrick Derrick, a leading character in the full–length novel *Love Among The Chickens*. A merchant prince who took to golf late in life, and lives for it, to the extent of running up for the Rockport Championship for each of the last two years. (**Vanfair–TEH**)

Claud Delamere and his drag queen

29

The Interlocking Grip

DERRICK, Genevieve: d. of **B Rockleigh Derrick**, waiting patiently for notification of a successful conclusion to the blackmail being perpetrated by her intended, **William Maxwell. (Vanfair–TEH)**

DETROIT: host to the American Amateur in what nearly became Jopp's Year. **(CCU–HEA)**

DEVINE, Raymond Parsloe: this rising young novelist is seen to rise a clear eighteen inches when a speeding golf–ball cleaves a new parting through his hair. Described by competent critics as more Russian than any other young English novelist, a fault for which he left **Wood Hills Literary and Debating Society** in disgrace and **Adeline Smethurst** to **Cuthbert Banks. (CCU–COC)**

DIBBLE, Ferdinand: though but a dub, a goof and a goop, is successful in defeating the man who tries to catch his golf–ball off his guard, the Cat Stroker, the Whip Cracker, the Heart Bowed Down and the Soup Scooper, and walks over all their faces with spiked shoes. Loves **Barbara Medway**, has neglected to ask if the feeling is returned, but is eventually emboldened to fold her in his arms, using the interlocking grip. **(HOG–THG)**

DIOGENES (412–323BC): forecast the emotions of a player at the water hole:

Be of good cheer. I see land.

(HOG–Preface)

DIPSOMANIAC: according to **Betty Weston**, someone who walks in her sleep. **(CCU–AMT)**

DISAFFECTION: reared its ugly head at **Wallace Chesney**'s plus fours. **(HOG–MPF)**

DIVORCE: The **Oldest Member**'s thesis is that most spring from husbands' too markedly superior prowess at golf, which results in due course in unpardonable revelations about the quality of her mashie shots. **(HOG–RFQ)**

31

DIX, Charlotte: unfeelingly wonders why people pay good money at the circus when they can watch **Wallace Chesney** trying to get out of the bunker by the eleventh green. **(HOG–MPF)**

DIX, Dorothy: an agony aunt to whom **Celia Todd** might have written, using the pseudonym "Perplexed". **(Cosmo–IGY)**

DIXON, Otis: must have changed his name to Rupert. **(Colliers–OBG)**

DIXON, Rupert: tactless and unpleasant young man, but has an equable golfing temperament. **(CCU–OBG)**

DONAH: "Never introduce your donah to a pal" represent six words containing the wisdom of the ages, and come to the rescue of the **Oldest Member** when **Mortimer Sturgis** was enthusing over the prospect of the explorer **Eddie Denton** meeting his fiancée **Betty Weston**. **(McClure–AMT)**

But the expression is reputed to have seven words in another place. **(CCU–AMT)**

DOUBLE–V: grip used by **Sir Hugo Drake** in preference to the **Vardon**. **(DOS; GOO)**

DRAKE, Sir Francis (c1540–1596): according to the **Oldest Member**, if he had been playing golf instead of bowls, he would have ignored the Armada altogether. **(HOG–ARP)**

DRAKE, Sir Hugo: stout doctor, uncle of **Bill Bannister/Bill Paradene**, capable of taking between four and twenty–seven at the eighteenth hole at **Bingley–on–Sea** and lessons from **Dr Smith**, and of foozling off the golf course. **(DOS, GOO)**

DROWNING:

> "If all misunderstandings are cleared away and nothing can come between us again, it is a small price to pay — unpleasant as it will be when it comes."

32

Sir Hugo's lesson

33

"Perhaps it will not be very unpleasant. They say
that drowning is an easy death."

"I didn't mean drowning, dearest. I meant a cold
in the head."

(MLF–WIH)

DUBBO: had it been used by **Agnes Flack**, each of **Smallwood Bessemer, Sidney McMurdo** and **Celia Todd** might have regretted the fact. **(Cosmo–IGY)**

DUCHY OF LANCASTER, Chancellor of: rang in a bad half–crown on the **First Gold Stick in Waiting**. **(NSE–FOC)**

DUNCAN, George: his proneness to waggle is disputed. **Chester Meredith** believes he waggles but little, and that he has **Felicia Blakeney** as a disciple, but **Pennefather** claims he waggles quickly and strongly. The **Oldest Member** says it is ideal for the hay–fever sufferer to imitate. Author of *On the Divot*. **(HOG–CFO,MPF; CCU–ROS; NSE–RHR)**

EARWIGS:

"Talking of earwigs, Miss Kent," he said, in a low
musical voice, "have you ever been in love?"

(HOG–ARP)

EAST BAMPTON: US seaside resort with ice–cream stands, hot doggeries and rescuers of drowning females, where **Agnes Flack** loses her outsize heart to a happy wanderer. **(NSE–FOC)**

EDGAR: see **Swan**.

EDWARD: Joe Poskitt's dog, which lost hair off its ribs from **Wilmot Byng**'s incessant patting. **(LEO–LEL)**

EGGS: see **Ham**.

34

EGYPT: where in a previous incarnation **Cora Spottsworth** was **Cleopatra** and **Sidney McMurdo** was **Antony**. And a country, one assumes, whose golf courses have more sandy wastes than grassy fairways. **(NSE–FOC)**

EIFFEL TOWER: mistaken by **George Mackintosh** for a niblick. **(CCU–SGM)**

ELIZABETH I, Queen (1533–1603): would have been out of place at **Woollam Chersey.** **(DOS; GOO)**

ELLERTON: a **Marois** or, maybe, **Marvis, Bay** youth, always in love with someone. **(MLF–WIH)**

ETERNITY: James Braid once said to **J H Taylor** that lucky twos seem like a dome of many–coloured glass to stain the white radiance of. **(LEO–FTL)**

EVE, Curse of: having to bear anecdotes from the men they love. **(CCU–SGM)**

EXCELSIOR: an expression used to indicate that no business could result. **(NSE–EXC)**

EYE, One Awful: when informed as a child that, watched his every movement and saw his every act, the **Oldest Member** suffered from self–conscious panic. **(CCU–SGM)**

FARRELL, Johnny: advises playing a chip shot as a crisp hit with the clubhead stopping at the ball and not following through. **(PLP–SLT)**

FATHEADS, Nature's Class 'A': **William Bates** is seen as one of. **(HOG–JGO)**

FARMER, Professor Pepperidge: author of *Sleepy Time*, given the pseudonym Count Dracula by **Patricia Binstead**. Face gaunt, lined and grim, with sinister, burning and literally hypnotic eyes, which obtain him a five thousand dollar advance. **(PLP–SLT)**

FELIX THE CAT: a series of humorous drawings on the lines of, sent **Pilcher** to the **Agnes Flack** residence in search of a model. (**MMS–PTT**)

FIGARO: laughs so he may not weep. (**DOS; GOO**)

FIRST GOLD STICK IN WAITING: received a bad half–crown. (**NSE–FOC**)

FIRST GRAVEDIGGER, the: the painstaking member of the **Wrecking Crew**, who did the shot of a lifetime in emulating **Chester Meredith**'s superb brassie–biff, with a shot that sent the ball breasting the hill like an untamed jack–rabbit of the Californian prairie, but landed straight in the seat of Chester's plus fours. (**HOG–CFO; LEO–LEL**)

FISHER, Bradbury: one of America's most promising tainted millionaires, suffering under a static handicap of twenty–four and having a wife who did not understand him, a degree from **Sing Sing** as student number 8,097,564 and a palatial home at **Goldenville, Long Island**, the twin crowns of whose perfections are his own collection of golf relics and **Blizzard**, the English butler whom his wife has purloined from the services of the **Duke of Bootle**. A crisis is precipitated when, in his wife's absence, he is offered a priceless golfing memento in exchange for Blizzard. Nevertheless, he loves his **Evangeline**, even though at one time, if he had lost a wife, he would have felt philosophically that there would be another one along in a minute. Cracked one hundred for the first time two weeks into his campaign of deception against his wife, and then won the competition for the sixth sixteen at the **Squashy Hollow Golf Club** Invitation Tournament. (**HOG–HST,KIW**)

FISHER, Evangeline: has never nursed a dear gazelle but, if she did, her sentiments towards it would be identical with those of her attitude to her English butler **Blizzard**. The most spirited of **Bradbury**'s five wives to date, but a golfing giggler, an elaborate waggler, likely to come out on the links in high heels at any time. (**HOG–HST,KIW**)

FITCH: who now can explain what it was that first attracted **Abercrombie?** (GWT-WOW)

FITCH, Clarice: see **Plinlimmon, Clarice.**

FLACK, Agnes: fine, large, handsome, 160lb, and all muscle; built on the lines of **Pop-Eye the Sailor Man**, and could have stepped into the role of Boadicea in a pageant. The idea of stealing her was rather like the notion of sneaking off with the Albert Hall. A capable swimmer, who gets annoyed when towed shorewards with her head under water. Did the short third at **Squashy Hollow** in one. A scratch player herself, she boasted that she could make a scratch player out of a cheesemite which had not lost the use of its wits. Novelist, so far unpublished. Regularly engaged to **Sidney McMurdo**, with whom she broke for various tempestuous reasons, and was engaged additionally to

Jack Fosdyke	(NSE-FOC)
Smallwood Bessemer	(NSE-TAH)
Harold Pickering	(FQO-SCM)
Cyril Grooly	(PLP-SLT)

and reneged on a promise to marry the winner of a match between **John Gooch** and **Frederick Pilcher.**

The late Dr J H C Morris drew attention in his book *Thank You, Wodehouse* (1981, Weidenfeld & Nicolson) to the problem of determining whether Agnes was English (as appears certain in **PTT**) or American (**FOC** and **TAH**) and concluded that she changed her domicile as regularly as she changed her fiancés. And strangely, Sidney McMurdo seemed to follow her whim!

What power is wielded by the heroines in Wodehouse's world. (MMS-PTT)

FLACK, Josiah: uncle of **Agnes**, his only surviving relation; a man with a deep sense of family obligations, more money than you could shake a stick at, one foot in the grave, and a property at Sands Point where he acts as host to **Captain Jack Fosdyke**. (NSE–FOC)

FLESHO: Vincent Jopp is begged by one of his ex–wives to take, since it is guaranteed to produce firm, healthy flesh on sparsely–covered limbs in no time. **G K Chesterton** writes that for years he has used no other, a sentiment endorsed by Warwick Armstrong. (CCU–HEA; Strand–HEA)

FLICKER FILM CO, California: to which **Raymond Parsloe Devine** is relegated. (CCU–COC)

FLORIDA: Mortimer Sturgis married **Mabel Somerset** quietly in a little village church in, instead of the florid ceremony he had planned at St. Thomas's, Fifth Avenue. (GWT–SUH)

FORRESTER, Grace: has an impressive wrist action when killing wasps with a teaspoon at a picnic. But unsound on golf, which she describes as the silliest game ever invented, a game for children with water on the brain who weren't athletic enough for **Animal Grab**. (CCU–WOW)

FORSYTE, Soames: an integral component of the perceived character of **Chester Meredith**. (HOG–CFO)

FOSDYKE, Captain Jack: the nature of the commission he claims to hold is undetermined. He is not, apparently, an officer in the Salvation Army, though may at one time have been an auxiliary temporary official in a fire brigade. Knows his Gazeteer and is equally at home in Pernambuco, East Bampton or Aintree, and can rescue skilled swimmers as well as fight sharks. Resides (maybe) at Wapshott Castle, **Wapshott–on–the–Wap,** Hants, and has served his sovereign (perhaps) as **Deputy Master of the Royal Buckhounds.** His clean–cut face, perfect figure and clothes make a pronounced impression on girls, a feeling encouraged when he establishes their financial prospects as promising. But though scratch, he believes golf is only a game, and he is severely lacking in golfing spirit. (NSE–FOC, BCE–MOB)

FOTHERGILL, Jimmy: his 220–yard drive is observed by the **Oldest Member**. Licks the boots off (not of) **Ferdinand Dibble**, and is one of a pair playing **Rupert Blake** and the Vicar when the latter smashes his putter. (CCU–WOW; HOG–THG,CFO)

FRENCH, Eulalie: heroine of *The Purple Fan*, affected different people in different ways. Her appeal was missed by the **Oldest Member**, but to **Jane Bates** was the most fascinating creature she had ever encountered. **Rodney Spelvin** claimed to have drawn her from Jane, even though he had callously forgotten her. (HGO–JGO)

FRISBY, Nathaniel: is disapproved of. After winning a golf match, extols the virtues of croquet and wonders why more people — such as his recently vanquished opponent **George William Pennefather** — do not take it up. (HOG–MPF)

FROZEN HORROR, the: soubriquet given to **Sir George Copstone** by the American golfing fraternity. (NSE–EXC)

FRY, S H: though beaten in the final of the amateur championship by **Hutchings**, it was a creditable performance as he was already in his thirty–fifth year when he first held a club. (CCU–AMT)

GABRIEL, Archangel: would have been kicked by **Ramsden Waters** if, refreshed by three ginger ales, he had laughed mockingly when Ramsden played an air shot. (CCU–ROS)

GABLE, Clark (1901–1960): might benefit from tricks with string. (LEO–FTL)

GADARENE SWINE: forbears of the **Wrecking Crew**. (HOG–CFO)

GANDLE, Raymond: a sensitive golfer, advocates the incineration of **Wallace Chesney**'s plus fours by the Public Hangman. (HOG–MPF)

GARDNER, Erle Stanley (1889–1970): displaced by **W H Auden** as **Agnes Flack's** bedtime reading. **(Cosmo–IGY)**

GARGLING: the technical term for speaking in one of the lesser–known dialects of the Walla–Walla natives of Eastern Uganda. **(CCU–AMT)**

GENEVIEVE: fiancée to an anonymous club member, a new light comes into her eyes when she takes six sloshes to cover fifty yards. **(CCU–ROS)**

GENGHIS KHAN (1162–1227): like **Attila the Hun,** would have seemed mild and spineless if he had sung the passage about birds nests in the hair from *Only God Can Make a Tree*. **(LEO–ALG)**

GIBBON, Edward (1737–1794): on finishing his *Decline and Fall of the Roman Empire* felt somewhat filleted for a while. **(FQO–SCM)**

GOBI DESERT: arid and monotonous, like **Clarice Fitch's** future. **(LEO–ALG)**

GOLF CLUBS

1 — THE INSTRUMENTS

The weapons used by **The Oldest Member**'s friends are generally referred to by their traditional names, rather than their modern equivalent. A certain amount of historical information concerning the development of the clubs can be derived from that fount of knowledge, *The Encyclopaedia Britannica*. It tells us first, that a putting cleek was a putter having an iron head on a wooden shaft. We also learn that by 1887, a well-equipped player would expect to carry:

Play club	For driving
Long spoon	For a hanging or rough lie
Short spoon	For shots within a hundred yards of the green
Brassie	Brass–soled to protect the club–head
Sand–iron	For bunkers and other hazards, and for lofting balls over stymies
Cleek	For long shots (the term originally referred to any iron–headed club, but became the Scots name for the No 1 or Driving iron)
Niblick (or track iron)	A small club with a heavy iron head for getting balls out of cart ruts or tough whins.

Numbered clubs began to be introduced between the wars when significant improvements were made to the shafts — high carbon steel that could be heat-treated and tempered replaced hickory, and shafts of fibre glass and aluminium were introduced. These numbered clubs were more finely graduated than the names which were traditionally used, and the shafts could be tailored to different specifications for flexibility and the point of flex.

It is possible to attempt roughly comparable lists of ancient and modern clubs, but even *The Encyclopaedia Britannica* was not fully capable of placing accurately all the Master's inventions!

WOODEN CLUBS

Modern	Ancient
1	Driver
2	Brassie, Brassy or Brassey
3	Spoon
4	Baffie or Baffy
5	Cleek

IRONS

Modern	Ancient
1	Driving iron or cleek
2	Mid iron
3	Mid Mashie
4	Mashie iron
5	Mashie
6	Spade mashie
7	Mashie niblick
8	Pitching niblick
9	Niblick
10	Sand wedge or pitching wedge

PUTTER

References to the following clubs can be found in the stories covered by this review, those in italics being found also in the comparative list above.

Baffy	used by Bobby Jones in the Infants' All–In Championship of Atlanta, Georgia, open to those of both sexes not yet having finished teething	**(HOG–HST)**
Braid iron		**(CCU–WOW)**
Brassey	a wooden club	**(CCU–ROS)**
Cleek	patent Sturgis aluminium self– self–compensating putting	**(CCU–AMT)**
Cleek	cut–down	**(CCU–WOW)**
Cleek	patent wooden–faced	**(CCU–AMT)**
Croquet mallet	to be used as putter	**(CCU–AMT)**
Driver		**(CCU–AMT)**
Driving– mashie	wooden–faced, weighing two pounds	**(HOG–MPF)**
Jigger		**(CCU–SUH)**
Mashie		**(CCU–WOW)**
Mashie–niblick		**(CCU–WOW)**
Niblick		**(CCU–WOW)**
Niblickski	according to Brusiloff	**(CCU–COC)**

No 3 iron   **(NSE–RHR)**

Putting cleek   **(CCU–AMT)**

Spoon   **(CCU-WOW)**

The Oldest Member at ease at one of his Home Courses

GOLF CLUBS

2 — THE COURSES

The following courses can be found in the oeuvre:

Aiken	Scene of PGW's only personal triumph on the golf course	**(The Golf Omnibus)**
Auchtermuchtie	Home club of Tammas McMickle	**(CCU–SUH)**
Detroit	Scene of the American Amateur in the year of Vincent Jopp's attempt	**(CCU–HEA)**
East Bampton		**(NSE–FOC)**
Goldenville	Long Island, NY, scene of the match for high stakes between Bradbury Fisher and J Gladstone Bott	**(HOG–HST)**
Little–Mudbury–in–the–Wold	Where Amanda Trivett's fiancé won a medal	**(CCU–LOH)**
Manhooset Golf & Country Club		**(GWT–SUH)** **(Colliers– OBG)**
Marois Bay	In reality, Marvis Bay	**(MLF–WIH)**
Marshy Moor		**(HOG–PRS)**
Marvis Bay	A hotel links, a sort of Sargasso Sea into which had drifted all the pitiful flotsam and jetsam of golf	**(HOG–THG)** **(CCU–OBG)**

Mossy Heath	Where Jane took eighty–two, not eighty–three, for a single hole	**(HOG–RFQ)**
Mount Pleasant, Cape Pleasant	Archibald Mealing v Mr Gossett	**(MUP–ARB)**
Nijni–Novgorod		**(CCU–COC)**
Oom		**(CCU–COG)**
Outer Isles		**(CCU–COG)**
Prestwick	Scene of the first open in 1860	**(CCU–OBG)** **(PLP–SLT)**
Rockport		**(TEH)**
Sound View	The main real source for the Oldest Member stories	
Southampton, Long Island	Where PGW used regularly to play a round	**(HOG–intro)**
Squashy Heath		**(FQO–SCM)**
Squashy Hollow	An American course on which Bradbury Fisher wins his first championship — the competition for the sixth sixteen at the Invitation Tournament	**(HOG–KIW)** **(NSE–FOC)** **(PLP–SLT)**
Windy Waste		**(HOG–PRS)**

| Wissahicky Glen | Scene of Vincent Jopp's rapid progress to scratch | (CCU–HEA) |
| Woodhaven | A combined golf club and tennis club | (Strand–WOW) |

GOLFING TERMS

Address	The waggle and stance before you make a stroke	(CCU–WOW)
Ancient mariner	A work which occurs to young men who are about to be regaled by the Oldest Member with one of his stories	(HOG–THG)
Ball	Part of the equipment required by those aspiring to play the game	(CCU–HEA)
	"One ball?"	
	"Certainly. What need is there of more?"	
Damnation	An expression used to indi-cate that a club, whizzing down, has brushed the surface of the rubber sphere, toppled it off the tee and propelled it six inches with a slight slice	(CCU–AMT)
Divots	Parts of the course which have to be replaced with meticulous care and an almost religious fervour when scooped up along with the ball	(HOG–KIW)
Dub	One who is capable of govern-ing an empire but fails to control a small white ball which presents no difficulties whatever to others with one ounce more brain than a cuckoo–clock	(HOG–THG)

Foozle	Make an error of consider-able magnitude,whether it be a slice, a top, or a press	(*passim*)
Goof	One of those unfortunate beings who have allowed the noblest of sports to get too great a grip on them, who have permitted it to eat into their souls, like some malignant growth Goofs brood and become morbid at their failures, so that even the Oldest Member may advise them to give up golf	(HOG–THG)
Goop	A man who's in love with a girl and won't tell her so. The girl can't be expected to fling herself into his arms unless he gives some sort of hint that he's ready to catch her	(HOG–THG)
Green	**George Parsloe** suggests they are so called because they are green	(HOG–THG)
Meat	Another term for *Green*	(HOG–MPF)
Putt	The one or more shots taken on a green to sink the ball in the hole. Normally played with a putter, **James Todd** finding that inadvertent use of the niblick did not fail to exercise a prejudicial effect on his game	(CCU–WOW)

Rubicon	The dividing–line that separates the golfer from the non–golfer, coming immediately after his first good drive	(CCU–AMT)
Scratch	A modern Quest equivalent to the search for the Holy Grail	(CCU–SUH)
Simp	See **Zimp**	(SatEvePost–PRS)
Tee	**Barbara Medway** wondered why they were so called	(HOG–THG)
Zimp	A trainee golfer who thinks that the tighter you hold a club the more force you get into the shot	(HOG–PRS)

GOLF–GERM: ran up **Rodney Spelvin**'s spine and bit him in the neck. **(HOG–PRS)**

GOLINSKY: not the real name of **Cyril Grooly**. **(PLP–SLT)**

GOOCH, Gloria: is fortunately situated in the matter of paying visits to libertines, since her scholarly husband spends nearly all his time in a library a hundred yards long. **(HOG–PRS)**

GOOCH, John: a writer of mystery stories and eighteen–handicap golfer required by **Agnes Flack** to play a match for her hand against **Frederick Pilcher**. His interest in her was not soully, but solely in the possibility of using her psychology in a series of stories entitled *Madeline Monk, Murderess.* **(MMS–PTT)**

GOOCH, Mortimer: a pusillanimous golfer who scratches in the semi–final round of the President's Cup for the fantastic reason that he has sprained an ankle. **(NSE–EXC)**

GOOD MORNING: when uttered by **Sally Smith** means that she loves. **(DOS; GOO)**

GORGON: imitated successfully by **Mrs Milsom**. **(MUP–ARB)**

GORILLA, Human: in line for a star appearance in *The Mystery of the Severed Ear.* **(MMS–PTT)**

GOSSETT: a broker in the City; a serpent in the Eden of **Cape Pleasant.** **(MUP–ARB)**

GOWF: the god which **the Pro** hopes to propitiate by apparently strange rites. **(CCU–COG)**

GRACE: rhymes with 'face'. **(CCU–WOW)**

GRAND VIZIER of OOM: adviser to the **King**, responsible for analysing the effect on the land of new religions. Rose to become Supreme Splendiferous Maintainer of the 24 Handicap except on Windy Days when it Goes up to 30. **(CCU–COG)**

GREENBEETLE, Mr: Timothy Spelvin's young friend. (NSE–RHR)

GREENS COMMITTEE: considered to run the club in the interests of the caddies (usually half-witted with pop eyes and 837 pimples), encouraging lost balls and going halves with them when they find and sell them. Or perhaps Committee members hang around trees and squeeze the cash out of them. In that way, they can afford to buy cars quicker than the makers can supply them, and their wives can go about in mink coats and pearl necklaces. They also extend holes into no man's land full of rocks, bushes, crevices, pots and pans so they can fill their sacks and buy their wives new shoes. (CCU–OBG)

GRIEF: automatically prevents pressing and over-swinging. (HOG–THG)

GRIM REAPER: to **Mortimer Sturgis**, the obstacle to immortality.

> "Will you fix up a match with me on the links of
> life which shall end only when the Grim Reaper
> lays us both a stymie?"

(CCU–SUH)

GROOLY, Cyril: junior partner of **Popgood & Grooly**, playing off a twenty-four handicap, and engaged to **Patricia Binstead**. (PLP–SLT)

GUBBO: a linament designed exclusively for the use of horses, inadvertantly recommended to **Agnes Flack** by **Smallwood Bessemer** for preventing stiffness, strains and soreness of the muscles. Its use by the trusting lady was the direct cause of her failure to win the Women's Club Championship. (**Cosmo–IGY**)

GUK: a word emitted in an odd strangled voice when a stricken **Bill Bannister**, looking like a prawn, advances a step towards **Sally Smith**. (DOS)

GUSSETT, Dr Ambrose: agreeable manners, frank blue eyes, an iodoform–scented butterfly until noting a marked cachexia in the presence of **Evangeline Tewkesbury**. Tries to learn to play tennis to advance his wooing, but ciné–kodak pictures of his first match generate much amusement. A doctor who gets exactly what the doctor ordered. **(NSE–UFD)**

GUTTY: the gutty (gutta–percha) ball is made from evaporated milky juice/latex of various South American and South Pacific Island trees. Around 1848 it replaced the feather ball (made of boiled feathers in leather) and was used until the rubber ball evolved around the beginning of the twentieth century. See **The Oldest Member**.

HACKENSCHMIDT: would have enthused professionally at **Jack Wilton**'s embrace of **Mary Campbell**. **(MLF–WIH)**

HAGEN, Walter: might have driven **Ambrose Gussett** off the tee. Advises putting off the left leg, and demonstrated the worth of his advice by holing a thirty–footer on an undulating green. **Cuthbert Banks** has often played with him. Author of *Hagen on Casual Water*. **(GWT–COC; NSE–UFD; DOS; GOO; SatEvePost–PRS)**

HALIBUT: a sardine's worst enemy, much to **Lord Tidmouth**'s distress. **(DOS; GOO)**

HAM: and **Eggs** compare to **Peter Willard** and **James Todd**. **(CCU–WOW)**

HAMLET: might have waggled, moodily, irresolutely, as **Jenkinson** waggled. **(HOG–THG)**

HEBER: the Israeli **George Mackintosh**. **(CCU–SGM)**

HEC, High Priest of: took the **Grand Vizier** aside to complain about the quality of meat being used for sacrifices. **(CCU–COG)**

HEMMINGWAY, Wadsworth: known to his fellow golfers as **Palsied Percy**, is a retired solicitor and one of those dark, subtle, sinister men who carry the book of rules in their bag and make it their best club. Not only a confirmed hole-claimer and Machiavellian schemer, but one with a way of suddenly clearing his throat on the greens which alone would ensure dislike. **(CCU–LOH; LEO–LEL)**

HENLEY, William Ernest (1849–1903): wrote about "the night that covers me, black as the pit from pole to pole." **(HOG–ARP)**

HENRIE, John:

> *To the immortal memory of*
> **JOHN HENRIE AND PAT ROGIE**
> *who at Edinburgh in the year*
> *A.D. 1593 were imprisoned for*
> *'Playing of the gowff on the links of*
> *Leith every Sabbath the time of*
> *the sermonses',*
> *also of*
> **ROBERT ROBERTSON**
> *who got it in the neck in*
> *A.D.1604 for the same reason.*

(CCU)

HIGGINBOTHAM, Edwin: business magnate, late second husband of **Lottie**, at the sound of whose theatrical tones he would shoot off to his club and seek to magnatise cotton. **(DOS)**

HIGGINBOTHAM, Lottie: née **Burke**, a friend of flashy appearance to **Bill Bannister**. Married twice, to Bixby and **Edwin Higginbotham**, the former converted into **Lord Tidmouth**, and the latter residing in Kensal Green Cemetary. **(DOS)**

HOLE IN ONE:

> "I did the pond hole in one. The ice was pretty thick and I used my iron. The pill skidded over it, jumped the bank, hit a frozen wormcast and popped into the hole. I've been missing those lately."

(McClure–SUH)

55

HOLMES, Mitchell: captivates the impressionable **Millicent Boyd** with his vocal sketch of a Pekingese quarrelling with a bulldog. On the links, however, his proficiency is apt to suffer from the uproar caused by the butterflies in the adjoining meadows. **(CCU–OBG)**

HOLY GRAIL: the equivalent to **Horace Bewstridge** was the **President's Cup**. **(NSE–EXC)**

HOME COURSE, The Oldest Member's: There remains considerable doubt as to how many courses can be regarded as **The Oldest Member**'s home course, as in his long career he has evidently been a member of more than one club, and has certainly lived in both the US and the UK. He is an enigmatic character, who appears to adopt the fisherman's approach to the facts, when it is necessary to tell a good story, and it does not help us when we are told on several occasions that the hole has been refashioned since the incident about to be related. This offers further evidence, it can be assumed, that some of the tales were enhanced in the telling, the claimed changes to the holes being part of the disguise used by the skilful raconteur. One way in which he avoided capture, of course, was to concentrate his narration on young persons, or those new to the club — in this way he had a clean tableau on which to weave his fabrications.

We do have some information about most of the holes at the Oldest Member's club from time to time, which is summarised below. The course is par 71; the course record, before Chester Meredith's assault on it, was 68; and Peter Willard's record in reverse is 161. Readers are recommended to consider this section in conjunction with the essay by the late Walter White, at Appendix 1, which describes how the holes were largely derived from a course at Sound View, Long Island, where Wodehouse played a lot from 1918 to 1921.

1st   even a topped shot will trickle a measurable distance down the hill, although there is a patch of rough halfway down.

2nd   (the eleventh before the course was redesigned); the lake hole, a short par 3, with a sandpit to the left of the flag.

3rd   par 4. Uphill all the way, with a deep ravine 50 yards from the tee. A tree, detached from the woods on the right, serves as a direction post, the flag being out of sight. A heap of stones twenty feet to the right of the tee, and sandbunkers to the left of the green.

4th   follows the curve of the road, on the other side of which are picturesque woods. A bunker spans the fairway.

5th   no information available.

6th   ground slopes from the tee, a dog–leg turn, and a large bunker to the left of the fairway.

7th   170 yards.

8th   sinister bunkers about the green, making the hole always tricky.

9th   the tee is on the farther side of the pond, beyond the bridge, where the water narrows almost to the dimensions of a brook. You drive across this water and over a tangle of trees and undergrowth on the other bank. The distance to the fairway cannot be more than 60 yards. It is then an uphill hole, with sinuous undulations of the green, a par 4.

10th over the brow of the hill, a par 4.

11th one of the trickiest; a little patch of wood on the right to catch the most slightly sliced drive.

12th long, slogging, dog-leg, par 5, with trees at the angle over which professionals use a spoon for their second to save a stroke.

13th 360 yards up a steep hill, with a long iron shot for the second and a blind green fringed with bunkers.

14th into a valley with the ground sloping sharply down to the ravine, set about with trees to catch a drive which is too straight.

15th longish hole, but straightforward up to the plateau green with its circle of bunkers.

16th perfectly plain hole with a broad fairway and a downhill run.

17th straightforward, but no other information available.

18th uphill run.

HONK-HONK: see **Poo-boop-a-doop.**

HOOK, Josh: golf-club Lothario who snares 'em by doing parlour tricks with string. **(LEO-FTL)**

HOPKINS, Harry Lloyd (1890-1946): played a friendly round with **Jack Fosdyke**. **(NSE-FOC)**

HOUDINI, Harry (1874-1926): might have been perplexed by the knot into which **Ramsden Waters's** vocal chords tied themselves. **(CCU-ROS)**

HUGGINS, Spike: noted safe-blower who shared the amenities of **Sing-Sing** with **Bradbury Fisher**, and model for Fisher's caddy. (**HOG-HST**)

HUMANITY: adjusts itself to conditions which at their outset appeared intolerable. (**HOG-MPF**)

HUTCHINGS, Mr C: an ex-amateur champion who did not start to play until he was past forty. (**CCU-AMT**)

INFANTS' ALL-IN GOLF CHAMPIONSHIP, The: of Atlanta, Georgia, is open to those of both sexes who have not yet finished teething. The contest is notable as having been **Bobby Jones'** first important competition. (**HOG-HST**)

INFLUENZA, Spanish: the germ of, not last in the popularity stakes. (**CCU-SGM**)

INTERLOCKING GRIP: as used by **Ferdinand Dibble** and **Barbara Medway**. (**HOG-THG**)

INVERLOCHTY: home of **Sandy McHoots**. (**CCU-HEA**)

ISISI, the: a tribe worshipping eight bearded gods. (**LEO-ALG**)

JAEL: wife of **Heber**. The most popular woman in Israel through acting on less provocation than **Celia Tennant**. (**CCU-SGM**)

JELLY-FISH: dislikes being sat upon.

> "There's a jelly-fish where you're going to sit," said Wilton.
>
> "I don't care."
>
> "It will. I speak from experience, as one on whom you have sat so often."

(MLF-WIH)

59

JENKINSON: a careworn, hopeless waggler, comparable to **Hamlet**, whose only chance of happiness lies in complete abstinence. A goof, whose goofery unfits him for the battles of life. **(HOG–THG)**

JENKINSON: like **Mr Burns**, considered by **Mrs Podmarsh** to set a poor example to his club colleagues. He is meant to be the best in the club but rarely manages to score eighty. **(Red–RPC)**

JEREMIAH: to fall out with whom meant that edging away was an advisable course of action. **(LEO–ALG)**

JOB: one of his chief trials was that his wife insisted on playing golf with him. **(HOG–KIW)**

JOHN, Augustus (1878–1961): of whom bobbed–haired females would ask **William Bates**'s opinion. **(HOG–JGO)**

JONATHAN: David and, compare to **Peter Willard** and **James Todd**. **(CCU–WOW)**

JONES, Robert Tyre ("Bobby") (1902–1971): many passing references to this revered master of the art. Was only slightly older than **Braid Bates** when he first played in the American Open. **(HOG–JGO)**

JOPP, Agnes Parsons: obtains a divorce decree against **Vincent Jopp** for persistent and aggravated mental cruelty, stating that, despite her tearful entreaties, he has repeatedly outraged her conjugal dignity and finer feelings by wearing a white waistcoat with a dinner jacket. **(CCU–HEA)**

JOPP, Jane Jukes: brings a successful action *a vinculis conjugii* against **Vincent Jopp** for calculated and inhuman brutality, deposing that he has repeatedly and categorically refused to take *Old Dr Bennett's Tonic Swamp Juice* three times a day. **(CCU–HEA)**

JOPP, Luella Mainprice: divorces **Vincent Jopp** for systematic and ingrowing fiendishness on the grounds that he does not like her in pink, and further, that he has twice, with malice aforethought, compelled her Pekingese dog **Tinky-Ting** to consume the leg of a chicken instead of the breast. **(CCU-HEA)**

JOPP, Thomas Reginald: a figment of the imagination to be christened in March. **(CCU-HEA)**

JOPP, Vincent: the rather engaging millionaire is probably real life's nearest approach to the tycoon of filmdom, whose jaw muscles jump when he is telephoning. Though still in his early thirties, has jumped off the dock early and often, scrambling back to shore via the divorce court lifebelt. Taking up golf in the same indomitable spirit which has won him his millions, he becomes scratch on his first morning, announces his intention of winning the American Amateur in his first season, and comes within a hole of doing so. **(CCU-HEA)**

JOSEPH: Felicia Blakeney's dog. **(HOG-CFO)**

JUDSON, Walter: like Petruchio's horse, might be said to be begnawn with the botts — in his case **Ponsford** and **Lavender B**. Stalwart and virile, eighteen handicap, a Fiend in human shape, who favoured the Sitting Hen putting method. **(FQO-JBW)**

JUKES, Alfred: capable of giving **Ernest Plinlimmon** ten and beating him. However, though technically a scratch man, is so lacking in golfing soul that he once returned to the club-house in the middle of a round because there was a thunderstorm and his caddie got struck by lightning. **(LEO-ALG; NSE-EXC)**

JUKES, Arthur: underdog in a freak golf match over the longest hole in the world, with the world itself as the prize, but his last-gasp victory was undoubtedly hollow. **(CCU-LOH)**

JUKES, Cyril: younger generation golfer whose habit of doing his round in the blizzard conditions of November gales meets with the approval of the **Oldest Member**. His wife, however, approved less, particularly when he was accompanied by her brother, who became bright blue with icicles forming on him. **(NSE-FOC)**

JUKES, Mrs: regards **Cyril** as a fat–headed sadist. **(NSE–FOC)**

JUKES, Otis: takes **Arthur**'s place in the American version of the long hole story. **(GWT–LOH)**

JUKES, Walter: bore a remarkable resemblance to **Walter Judson**, particularly in relation to an affliction with the **Botts**. But in Walter Jukes's case, it was **Horace Botts** who caddied in his match against **George Prosser**, and demonstrated a considerable propensity to annoy. **(JohnBull–KYT)**

JUKES, ENDERBY & MILLER LTD: florists, who respectfully inquire whether **William Bates** wishes them to renew his esteemed order to them to deliver one b. of white violets annually. **(HOG–JGO)**

JULIET: Grace Forrester's cousin, mother of **Willie** amongst others. **(CCU–WOW)**

KADDIZ: slaves granted to **the Pro** at **Oom** and other worshippers of the new religion.

> "I have often felt that it would be a relief to one's feelings to sacrifice one or two *kaddiz*, but **the Pro** for some reason or other has set his face against it."

(CCU–COG)

KARLOFF, Boris (William Henry Pratt, ed. Dulwich College) (1887–1969): on one of his bad mornings, resembled **Prof Farmer**. **(PLP–SLT)**

62

Kaddiz!

63

KEATS: wrote mistakenly about stout **Cortes** (or **Cortez**) staring with eagle eyes at the Pacific. What he said in *On First Looking into Chapman's Homer* was:

> Then felt I like some watcher of the skies
> When a new planet swims into his ken;
> Or like stout Cortez, when with eagle eyes
> He stared at the Pacific — and all his men
> Look'd at each other with a wild surmise —
> Silent, upon a peak in Darien.

What he should have said, according to the anonymous correspondent who wrote to Wodehouse on the subject after the story appeared in the *Saturday Evening Post* was that it was Balboa rather than Cortez who performed this feat. Wodehouse dismissed this point in the positive manner he always sought to use with critics, by pointing out that the Pacific was open for being stared at about that time, and he could see no reason why Cortez should not have had a look as well.

(CCU–WOW)

KENT, Mary: daughter of an old school–friend of **Mrs Podmarsh** come to stay for the autumn and winter, playing off twelve. **(HOG–ARP)**

KISS–IN–THE–RING: a more athletic game than golf. **(GWT–WOW)**

KNOPP, Lord Knubble of: recipient of **Slythe & Sayle**'s confidences. **(NSE–FOC)**

LAMOUR, Dorothy (b 1914): did not return **Irwin Botts'** affections. **(NSE–EXC)**

LEIGH: a village too small for both **Arthur Jukes** and **Ralph Bingham**. **(CCU–LOH)**

LENIN (Vladimir Ilyich Ulyanov) (1870–1924): plays golf with **Trotsky** against **Brusiloff** and the Pro on the **Nijni Novgorod** course. **(CCU–COC)**

LINX: the outdoor temple of the god **Gowf**. (CCU–COG)

LITTLE HAWLEY: a bad shot with the brassey at, may teach prudence and provide unwanted practice with the niblick. (CCU–LOH)

LITTLE-MUDBURY-IN-THE-WOLD: a championship course as far as **Amanda Trivett**'s fiancé is concerned. (CCU–LOH)

LLOYD GEORGE, David, (1st Earl Lloyd–George of Dwyfor) (1863– 1945) : meets **Brusiloff**. (CCU–COC)

LONG HOLE, the: a sudden death match between **Arthur Jukes** and **Ralph Bingham**, over approximately sixteen miles, with the whole world as the prize. It started at the first tee, was to finish in the doorway of the Majestic Hotel in Royal Square. The players used such assistance as they could legally find on the way, including flat-bottomed boats, small cars driven by grimy young men in sweaters, casual dogs and small messenger–boys. Despite two respected umpires who accompanied them, neither player improved his reputation for playing the game in the correct spirit, and the verdict on the game given by the third umpire was as appropriate in the circumstances as could be imagined. (CCU–LOH)

LOUIS QUINZE: catalyst for **Bradbury Fisher**'s bed and library at Goldenville. (HOG–HST,KIW)

LOVE:

I doubt if golfers ought to fall in love. (FQO–SCM)

* * *

"Isn't he a darling!" she said, addressing the Oldest Member.

The Sage cast a meditative eye upon the infant. Except to the eye of love, it looked like a skinned poached egg. (CCU–ROS)

"He's in love."

"You think so?"

"I'm sure of it. I noticed it the day I arrived here.
I had begun to tell him about the long brassie–shot
I made at the sixteenth hole and he gave a sort of
hollow gasp and walked away."

"Walked away?"

"Walked away in the middle of a sentence. The
boy's in love. There can be no other explanation."

(DOS; GOO)

LOVERS' LEAP: together with the waterfall, the view from the Eighth Green and **Wallace Chesney**'s plus fours, something not to be missed when visiting the course. **(HOG–MPF)**

LUCAS, George: wagered half–a–dozen of ginger ale on **Grace Forrester**'s intentions, confidently assuming that no girl could love a man with calves like **James Todd**, particularly if he had the bad taste to insist on displaying them to all and sundry under knickerbockers. **(CCU–WOW)**

LUMMOX, the big: **Agnes Flack**'s pet name for **Sidney McMurdo**. **(FQO–SCM)**

MACBEAN, Sandy: author of *How to Become a Scratch Man from your First Season by Studying Photographs.* **(CCU–WOW)**

MACDONALD: see **McClurg**.

MACKINTOSH, George: a man of no vices save a tendency to use the mashie for shots which need the light iron, develops a gift of the gab capable of stopping the Cornish Riviera Express on its way to Penzance, cured by the judicious use of a niblick. **(CCU–SGM)**

66

His friends might have rescued him earlier by had they a Jeevesian insight into the psychology of the individual. **Lord Tidmouth** told the story of a ventriloquist who used to annoy his wife by having long conversations with himself in his sleep. But by the greatest of good fortune, one day he caught himself cheating at patience, and never spoke to himself again. A not dissimilar solution must surely have been Plan B if the niblick had failed. **(GOO)**

MAH–JONG: William Bates's teeth–gnashing exercises were mistaken for the sound of the game's counters, when played by **Braid Bates**. **(HOG–PRS)**

MAINWARING, Claude: George Mackintosh can give him a third and beat him easily. **(CCU–SGM)**

MANDERS, Kitty: friend of **Eunice Bray** who frequently showed how proud she was of the small silver cup she won at a monthly handicap, receiving 36. **(CCU–ROS)**

MANHOOSET: won't seem the same without **James Todd**. Location of a fine Golf and Country Club. **(GWT–WOW; OBG)**

MAN WITH THE HOE, the: member of the **Wrecking Crew**. **(LEO–LEL)**

MAPLEBURY, Lora Smith: millionaire **Bradbury Fisher**'s fifth mother–in–law, who was every bit as objectionable as the first four, and to whose neck, given a free hand, he would have tied a brick before dropping her in the water hazard at the second. Had a sniff which could crack a coffee cup, but despite this handicap found nothing wrong in mistrusting Bradbury because he wiggled the tip of his nose. She would decidedly not have done for the Duke. **(HOG–KIW)**

MARCUS AURELIUS (or perhaps AURELIUS, Marcus) (121–180): according to the **Oldest Member**, the golfer should imitate the spirit of, as expressed in *Meditations*:

"Whatever may befall thee, it was preordained for thee from everlasting. Nothing happens to anybody which he is not fitted by nature to bear."

"That which makes the man no worse than he was makes life no worse. It has no power to harm, without or within."

The Oldest Member deduced from these words a number of telling facts — that Marcus was a golfer, indeed a bad golfer. That he had had putts stopping on the edge of the hole. That he rarely went round in under a hundred and twenty (*centum et viginti*, CXX). And that the niblick was his club. **(CCU–OBG)**

MARIE: Lottie Higginbotham/**Burke**'s maid, who needs to have a safe pair of hands. **(DOS; GOO)**

MARKS–MORRIS GLUE FACTORY: an obliging telephone operator, possibly a former courier to a travel agency, connects **Jane Bates** with, instead of to **Rodney Spelvin**. **(HOG–PRS)**

MAROIS BAY: resort with golf links and tennis courts, but a fictional place even by fictional standards, having only appeared courtesy of not an author but a Methuen type–setter or proof–reader. When the story *Wilton's Holiday* appeared in the July 1915 issue of *Strand*, its setting was explicitly stated to be Marvis Bay, but for some reason, which will probably never be known, this was not considered sufficiently exclusive by the particular Methuen employee when it first appeared in *The Man With Two Left Feet*. And the editors of most, if not all, later editions, instead of staring in bewilderment and thinking that this is where they score a point or two off their trade rivals, have allowed their innate conservatism to perpetuate the fallacy that Marois Bay exists. The Americans have to be excused from this general condemnation — showing consummate good sense, the editor of the American edition refused to include the story and thus ensured he would not be tarred with the same brush. **(MLF–WIH)**

MARSHY MOOR: a course where **Reginald Brown** had a little experience. (**HOG–PRS**)

MARVIS BAY GOLF AND COUNTRY CLUB: where the **Oldest Member** rested in a rocking chair. The identification of the course (or, since he tells many of his stories to American audiences also, courses) where the OM normally resided is tricky, as it is only occasionally, as in **CCU–OBG**, that any clues are given. And an exactly opposite hint is given in **HOG–THG**, in which it is clear that Marvis Bay is not the home course. The descriptions we have of the various holes imply that the OM's regular course, and Marvis Bay in **CCU–OBG**, are one and the same. The conclusion that the OM must have moved away before the action of **HOG–THG** is not valid, since Marvis Bay in that story is a hotel links full of the dregs of the golfing world. The only solution seems to be that the OM's course is indeed Marvis Bay, a sort of major regional centre, with the tourist resort of Marvis Bay and its hotels some miles distant, and actually on the coast. But the map of the area remains unclear.

Some of the Mafia demonstrate their styles

MARVIS BAY MAFIA: the dregs of the golfing world — stout middle-aged men who, after a misspent youth devoted to making money, had taken to golf and pursued nightmare styles to which they owed their names:

Cat–Stroker	who addressed his ball as if he were stroking a cat
Heart Bowed Down	who brooded over each shot like one whose heart is bowed down by bad news from home
Snake–Killer	who wielded his mid–iron like one killing snakes
Soup–Scooper	who scooped with his mashie as if he were ladling soup
Whip–Cracker	who drove as if he were cracking a whip
and one man	who was so bad that no name could be found adequately to describe his attempt to deceive his ball and lull it into a false sense of security by looking away from it and then making a lightning slash in the hope of catching it off its guard.

This miserable coterie was managed by an octogenarian, his badge of office an ear–trumpet, who was addicted to buns and milk. **(HOG–THG)**

The Octogenarian

MARVIS BEACH: on the south coast of England, a meeting point for those skilled in medical arts, and with a links where it is possible to spot **Sally Smith** performing. **(GOO)**

MASSY, Arnaud: when he won the Open, one of the features of his play was a sort of wiggly twiggle at the top of his swing which added yards to his drive. **(MMS-PTT)**

MATILDA, Lady: a drag queen. **(CCU-ROS)**

MAXWELL, William John: wins **Genevieve**, d. of **B Rockleigh Derrick**, despite stunted income, through the clever use of psychology. It amounted to blackmail of the "Your blessing or the Championship" variety, and was consummately successful following a final act one inch from the cup at the eighteenth. **(TEH)**

McBEAN, Sandy: author of *How to Become a Scratch Player Your First Season by Studying Photographs.* Not to be confused with **Sandy MacBean. (CCU-ROS)**

McCAY: secretary of the **Cape Pleasant** club. A chartered accountant and stout, so romantic and sentimental. Knew **Ella Wheeler Wilcox** by heart, and could take **Browning** without anaesthetic. Plotted with **Sigsbee** and others before losing to **Mealing. (MUP-ARB)**

McCLURG: and **MacDonald**, of 18 West Street, for all golfing supplies, or you can find a branch at 18 W 49th Street. **(CCU-LOH; GWT-LOH**

McCOY, the Real

Wodehouse used the names of many real life golfers in his stories, usually as role models for the club members. Many have apparently written books (see Appendix 2); others have a characteristic method of addressing or hitting the ball and yet another group are mentioned in their role as tournament winners.

The following table summarises the achievements of those authentic golfers who have won the UK or US Open or Amateur Championships, or the US Professional Championship. Edward Blackwell, S H Fry, Abe Mitchell and Ray Venturi do not qualify for inclusion in this list.

	UNITED KINGDOM		UNITED STATES		
	Amateur	Open	Amateur	Open	Professional
Braid, James		1901,05,06, 1908,10			
Duncan, George		1920			
Hagen, Walter		1922,24,28,29		1914,19	1921,24–27
Hilton, Harold	1900,01,11,13		1892,97	1911	
Hutchings, C	1902				
Hutchinson, Horace	1886,87				
Jones, Bobby	1930	1926,27,30	1924,25,27,28, 1930		1923,26,29, 1930
Lema, Tony		1964			
Massy, Arnaud		1907			

	UNITED KINGDOM		UNITED STATES		
	Amateur	Open	Amateur	Open	Professional
Morris, Tommy, Jnr		1868–70,72			
Morris, Tommy, Snr		1861,62,64,67			
Nicklaus, Jack		1966,70,78	1959,61	1962,67, 1972,80	1963,71,73, 1975,80
Palmer, Arnold		1961,62	1954	1960	
Park, Willie		1860,63,66,75			
Player, Gary		1959,68,74		1965	1962,72
Ray, Ted		1912		1920	
Taylor, John H		1894–95,1900 1909,13			
Travis, Walter T		1904	1900,01,03		
Vardon, Harry		1896,98,99 1903,11,14			

75

McHAGGIS, Jock: competed in the Open Golf Foursome in 1912.
(CCU–SUH)

McHEATHER, Andy: also competed in the Open Foursome in 1912.
(CCU–SUH)

McHOOTS, Sandy: one of Scotland's doughtiest golfers, won both the British and American Opens, and is looked up to in many stories. When engaged as private coach by **Vincent Jopp**, a non–player who aspires to win the Open in his first season, his salutary advice can be summarised as:

> "Ane: keep your heid still. Twa: keep your ee on
> the ba'. Thrree: dinna prress."

His spectacular plus fours were returned to **Cohen Bros** despite being made to measure.

(CCU–HEA,SGM,SUH; HOG–MPF,RFQ; MMS–PTT)

McMICKLE, Tammas: fourth in the Open of 1911, and the pro at **Auchtermuchtie,** who converts **Mabel Somerset**, the Ladies' Open Croquet champion, into a passable golfer. **(CCU–SUH)**

76

McMURDO, Sidney George: outsize golfer, 200lb, whose drive is as powerful as his jealousy, is a second vice–president of the **Jersey City and All Points West Mutual and Co–operative Life and Accident Insurance Company**. Next to **Agnes Flack** and his steel-shafted driver, he loves his second vice–presidency better than anything else in the world. When he first proposed to her on the sixth green the rumblings of her mirth were heard in the locker-room, causing two men who were nervous of thunderstorms to scratch their match. In his periods of being unengaged to Agnes, he acquires a number of other temporary fiancées, including

      Cora McGuffy Spottsworth   NSE–FOC

      Celia Todd   NSE–TAH

When hearing that Agnes had signed up with **Cyril Grooly**, the sound of his gnashed teeth was like that of castanets being manipulated by a Spanish Dancer. (**PLP–SLT**)

Sidney McMurdo attends Cora Spottsworth

Angus McTavish discovering the loss of sixpence

McTAVISH, Angus: though slight of build, can paste a golf ball 200 yards from the tee, to the admiration of all except **Legs Mortimer**. When caddying for **Evangeline Brackett**, he looked like a V–shaped depression off the coast of Ireland. True to his background, however, he loses his match against a hopeless foozler, **Robinson**, after being three up at the turn, when he discovers the loss of sixpence through a hole in his pocket. (**CCU–HEA; LEO–FTL**)

MEALING, Archibald: a golfing trier in whom desire outruns performance, incapable of doing a hole in single figures. Engaged to **Margaret Milsom**. Generally ordinary, attempts to inoculate him with a love of poetry while at school not having taken. (**MUP–ARB**)

MEASLES: golf, like, should be caught young. (**CCU–AMT**)

MECCA: reproduced, for golfers at least, at **Bingley–on–Sea**. (**DOS**)

MEDALLION–CARTERET, Sir Jasper: wore riding–boots to kick his girl with, before dragging her round the room by her hair. (**LEO–ALG**)

MEDWAY, Barbara: a girl golfer who is wholeheartedly approved by that stern critic, the **Oldest Member**. In his view, she carries the sunshine round the course with her. The object of **Ferdinand Dibble**'s unspoken love, with an affinity to **Marvis Bay** and a desire to hit her men on the head with something hard, heavy and with knobs on. (**HOG–THG**)

MENDELSSOHN'S WEDDING MARCH: a thousand birds trilled, in the trees above **Ferdinand Dibble** and **Barbara Medway**. (**HOG–THG**)

MEREDITH, Chester: believes certain human misfits, viz the **Wrecking Crew**, should not be allowed on any decent links. His unnatural reticence in the presence of **Felicia Blakeney** made her feel that marriage to him would be like marrying a composite of **Soames Forsyte, Sir Willoughby Patterne** and all her brother **Crispin's** friends. But the quality of his speech on the eighteenth in his record round (see **Oaths**) impressed her sufficiently to overcome her fears. (HOG–CFO)

MEROLCHAZZAR of OOM, King: in love, by correspondence course, with the **Princess of the Outer Isles**. (CCU–COG)

MERRIDEW, Amelia: is scheduled to become the fourth Mrs **Vincent Jopp**, and in trying to evade the honour gets herself arrested by two members of the Greens Committee. (CCU–HEA)

MESSMORE, Dwight: a pin–headed young string–bean of the tennis court, is **Ambrose Gussett**'s most formidable rival for the hand and heart of la **Tewkesbury**. So expert in outdoor ping–pong that he is able to celebrate with enthusiasm his nomination for the Davis Cup which also finishes his love game. (NSE–UFD)

MEZZANINE FLOOR: into which the **First Grave–Digger**'s lunches of fifty–seven years had caused his chest to slip. (HOG–CFO)

MGEEBO–MGOOPIES: chief plugged a **Fosdyke** eye before being the star attraction at a costly funeral. (NSE–FOC)

'MGOOPI 'MGWUMPI: the chief of the Lesser Mgowpi, with whom **Ernest Plinlimmon** is disadvantageously compared. (LEO–ALG)

MGUBO–MGOMPI's: last year's war–dance of the, produced song hits. Its chief was shot by **Jack Fosdyke**, for smirching the honour of the Fosdykes. (NSE–FOC)

MILLAY, Edna St Vincent (1892–1950): apparently not **Bugs Baer**. (NSE–TAH)

MILLENNIUM: must be set back indefinitely — until golf–clubs make it a rigid rule that no wife be allowed to play with her husband. With his classical background and clear analytical skills, Wodehouse would obviously not have fallen for the short–termism promoted by some politicians and journalists of the late twentieth century, but would have understood that, unless action were taken, the new millennium would arrive, on schedule, on January 1st, 2001. **(HOG–KIW)**

MILLER, Heloise: despite being loved by another, finds **Jack Wilton** interesting. Her golf round with **Teddy Bingley** caused a wallowing in misery. **(MLF–WIH)**

MILSOM, Margaret: **Archibald Mealing**'s fiancée, devoted apparently enthusiastically to various bards, and shows good taste in not monogramming forget–me–nots on tobacco–pouches. **(MUP–ARB)**

MILSOM, Mrs: not wrapped up in **Archibald Mealing**, generally crying bitterly when she saw him, and calling him "guffin" and "gaby" **(MUP–ARB)**

MILSOM, Stuyvesant: thought **Archibald Mealing** a bit of an ass, but in return for a couple of saffron–coloured bills was prepared to sit and listen to his mother on the subject. **(MUP–ARB)**

MONEY MARKET, Monarch of the: the stamp of the true, is the ability to switch a cigar from one corner of the mouth to the other without wiggling the ears. **(CCU–HEA)**

MONROE, Marilyn (1926–1962): outer crust bore strong resemblance to **Angela Pirbright**. **(FQO–JBW)**

MONTAGUES: see **Capulets**.

MONTROSE: to win or lose it all, says. **(DOS; GOO)**

MORDYKE, Carruthers: compared to **Ramsden Waters** when in chapter forty–one of his adventures, he flings from him **Ermyntrude Vanstone**. The novelist — whose identity is not revealed but who is surely (or shirley) a she — has a style that from even a short extract one can recognise as from the school of Rosie M Banks. **(CCU–ROS)**

MORRIS, Old Tom: to his marriage could be traced the existence of **Tommy Morris**. (CCU–SUH)

MORRIS, Tommy: winner of the British Open four times in succession. (CCU–SUH)

MORRISON, Alex: had the wrong angle on the game. (NSE–TAH)

Legs Mortimer's practical joke

MORTIMER, Legs: a life–and–soul–of–the–party serpent who held **Evangeline Brackett** like that, which might have been all right and might not. But surely it was not all right to call golf clubs hockey-knockers, to put down a soap–ball on the eighteenth, or to go round offering trick cigars to bishops. **(LEO–FTL)**

MOSEBY, Major: having been stone deaf since 1898, is now the only member who will go round the course with **'Gabby' George Mackintosh. (CCU–SGM)**

MOSSY HEATH GOLF CLUB: at whose seventh **Sandy McHoots**, on a stirring occasion, took eleven. That, with the fourth and the fifteenth, is the most poisonous hole on the course. The Ladies' Invitation Tournament at, is one of the most important fixtures of the local female golfing year. **(HOG–RFQ)**

MPHM: a Scottish expression used by the least loquacious, a group which includes the finest golfers. It is all that could be extracted from the illustrious **Sandy McHoots** when, on the occasion of his winning the British Open Championship, he was interviewed by reporters from the leading daily papers as to his views on Tariff Reform, Bimetallism, the Trial By Jury system and the Modern Craze for Dancing. (Having uttered which, he shouldered his bag and went home to tea.) **(CCU–SGM)**

MULLINER, a Devonshire: whose daughter married a man named Flack and was the only proficient golfing Mulliner. **(MMS–PTT)**

MULLINER, Mr: a tale–teller at the **Anglers' Rest**, whose family's exploits deserve a volume all to themselves. **(MMS–PTT)**

MURPHY, Dr: his Tonic Swamp Juice, to be taken three times a day after meals, is recommended for **Blizzard's** sciatica. **(HOG–HST)**

MURRAY, Arthur: a dream world of breathtaking beauty pirouetted before one as if he were teaching it dancing in a hurry. **(PLP–SLT)**

NAPOLEON (1769–1821): would not have amounted to anything if he had not curbed his fiery temper. But even he would have wilted if surrounded, like **Vincent Jopp**, by fussy and immature females to each of whom he once happened to have been married. A vision of him at St Helena was recalled to the minds of not a few members by the sight of **Angus McTavish**'s knitted brows and terrace–pacing. **Bill Bannister** looked at **Lord Tidmouth** as a young soldier at. **(CCU–OBG, HEA; LEO–FTL; DOS)**

NASTIKOFF: eminent modern Russian novelist, worse than **Sovietski**, is spitted of. **(CCU–COC)**

NATURE'S REMEDY: a locusts' nest two inches above the head. **(LEO–FTL)**

NERO (37–68): to describe **Ramsden Waters**'s soul one would need to combine the outstanding characteristics of, a wildcat and the second mate of a tramp steamer. **(CCU–ROS)**

NEW YORK, Bishop of: one of the prelates who would in normal circumstances have been expected to preside over the wedding of **Mortimer Sturgis** and **Mabel Somerset** at St Thomas's, Fifth Avenue. **(McClure–SUH)**

NIJNI–NOVGOROD: Brusiloff's home town, where the worst thing to happen was a brace of bombs coming in through the window and mixing themselves up with the breakfast egg. He played a memorable foursome with **Lenin, Trotsky** and the Pro. **(CCU–COC)**

NIMROD: author of the standard text–book on killing lions. **(CCU–COG)**

NINCTOBINKUS: a Holstein butter–churner. **(DOS)**

NINETY–NINE: the women in **Bill Bannister/Paradene**'s life do not amount to half as many as that. **(DOS; GOO)**

OAKES, OAKES & PARBURY Ltd: a considerate telephone exchange connects **Jane Bates** with this firm of fancy goods dealers. **(HOG–PRS)**

OATHS: to refrain entirely from, during a round, is almost equivalent to giving away three bisques. Those of **Chester Meredith** cannoned into each other, linked hands and formed parties, got themselves mixed up in weird vowel sounds, the second syllable of some red-hot verb forming a temporary union with the first syllable of some blistering noun. The result would have tested any competitor in a spelling bee:

"!!!!!!!!!!!!!!"

"—!—!!—!!!—!!!!—!!!!!"

"***!!!***!!!***!!!***!!!"

(HOG–CFO)

The authorities suggest that more than one eavesdropper took notes at the time. The alternative version of his speech runs like this:

"Hell!"

"—!—!!—!!!—!!!!—!!!!!"

"****! @§&%#!! $^{31}/_{42}$?$@#)*§!!!!"

(SatEvePost–CFO)

OCTOGENARIAN, an: manager of the **Marvis Bay Mafia**, he is nevertheless treacherously guilty of passing vital intelligence to the enemy in the shape of **Barbara Medway** whilst taking his bun and milk, into which Barbara would have dropped a beetle for no more than two pins. **(HOG–THG)**

OLDEST MEMBER, the: also known as **the Sage**. A Jekyll and Hyde personality, so much so that Dr J H C Morris has postulated four distinct personalities, three British and one American. He is at least seventy and claims not to have played golf since the rubber–cored ball superseded the old dignified **Gutty** in **CCU–OBG**, yet in **CCU–SGM** he apparently went round twice in one day. He was a Cambridge graduate in **CCU–HEA**, but in **LEO–LEL** he had been at Oxford with **Joseph Poskitt**. He has, of course, a calm and dreamy eye: the eye of a man who has seen Golf steady and seen it whole (or hole).

His attitude towards tennis players resembled that of Christians towards Ebonites, but that may have been in part because he was less successful in attaching himself to a pair of their lapels to illustrate with a reminiscence the silver lining to a problem being experienced by members of either sex at his home club. It would be wrong to describe him as a bore, except when he makes a major philosophical statement such as "Golf is the Great Mystery", because his stories are always entertaining, but it cannot be denied that the prospect of listening caused varying reactions, not uniformly enthusiastic, in the behaviour of the threatened recipients. **(passive)**

OLD FATHER TIME: member of the **Wrecking Crew**. **(LEO–LOL)**

ONGOs

Objects, whether animal, vegetable or mineral, encountered in the course of their duties by big game hunters. Examples include

bongo	wild animal, the male of which species is called a bull
dongo	undergrowth
gongo	animal which, when wounded, corners hunters
jongo	short–horned, native oxen, the staple food of the crocodile
kongo	pool
longo	rapids
mongo–mongo	disease, involving pink spots, known as the scourge of the West African hinterland
pongo	native bearer
tongo	narrow place for gongos to corner hunters
wongo	a sort of broth composed of herbs and meat–bones, as in the expression *"deposit oneself in the wongo"*
yongo	prowling creature, which frequents distant deserts
zongo	poisonous creature

(CCU–AMT)

OOM ARISTOCRACY, the:

  King Merolchazzar

  Grand Vizier

  Lord High Chamberlain

  Supreme Hereditary Custodian of the Pet Dog

  Exalted Overseer of the King's Wardrobe

  Keeper of the Eel-hounds

  Hereditary Bearer of the King's Baffy

  Second Deputy Shiner of the Royal Hunting Boots

  Second Tenor of the Corps of Minstrels

The clergy are not considered to hold such important positions. The leader of the priests of the sixty-seven gods of Oom was merely the **High Priest of Hec.** (CCU–COG)

OSBALDISTONE, Miss: cubist painter described as a manly young woman who calls on **Jane Packard** for cigarettes or, alternatively, cocaine, and who, like Jeeves on another notable occasion, lets the cat out of the bag concerning Eulalie. (**HOG–JGO**)

OSBORNE STADIUM: at **Sing Sing**, the opening ceremony of which, to be attended by former students, had to be postponed because of an outbreak of mumps in the prison. (**HOG–KIW**)

OTHELLO: would have retained but a slight edge over **Sidney McMurdo** in the matter of jealousy. (**NSE–FOC**)

OUIMET, Frankie: Bradbury Fisher croons over the pair of trousers in which the master won his historic replay against **Vardon** and **Ray** in the American Open. (**HOG–HST**)

OUTER ISLES, the Princess of the: stood on the terrace in the clear sunshine of the summer morning, looking over the King's garden. With her delicate little nose she sniffed the fragrance of the flowers. Her blue eyes roamed over the rose bushes, and the breeze ruffled the golden curls about her temples. Presently, she perceived a godlike man hurrying across the terrace, pulling up a sock. At the sight of him the Princess's heart sang within her like the birds in the garden and soon afterwards the King's heart joined hers in a duet. **(CCU–COG)**

PACKARD, Jane: calm, slow–moving like **William Bates**. But inclined to romance under the influence of **Luella Periton Phipps**, only returning to reality when advised by William to play her fourth shot at the seventh at Mossy Hill from where it floats. Accepted William's proposal whilst detaching a newt from her right ear. **(HOG–RFQ)**

PAGE BOY, a: at the Esplanade, **Marvis Beach**. Recommends vinegar. **(GOO)**

PALMER, Arnold: whose game **Prof Farmer** recommended **Cyril Grooly** to be hypnotised into imitating, in preference to Gary Player or Jack Nicklaus. But if these three were rolled into one with Tony Lema and Ray Venturi, the result would have been the hypnotised Grooly, in terms of confidence, at least. **(PLP–SLT)**

PALSIED PERCY: as **Wadsworth Hemmingway**, contests the President's Cup with **Joseph Poskitt**. **(LEO–LOL)**

PAMELA, Lady: caught a juicy one by **Sir Jasper Medallion–Carteret** and his hunting–crop. **(LEO–ALG)**

Bill Paradene is instructed to prod Sally Smith's legs

PARADENE, Bill: res. **Woollam Chersey, Hants**. Unofficially engaged to **Lottie Burke**, an attachment from which he wishes out, and from which he is unnecessarily bought out by his Uncle **Sir Hugo Drake**. Looks after a thousand pigs, which unexpectedly need milking, but which enable him to surprise **Sally Smith** into losing control of her vascular motors.

In **DOS**, his surname is given as **Bannister**, and Lottie has already been married twice, moving through the ranks of the Burkes and the Bixbys to the Higginbothams. **(GOO; DOS)**

PARADISE VALLEY: golfing holiday location for **Cyril Grooly**. **(PLP–SLT)**

PARK: see **Tilford**

PARK, Willie: won the first Open at Prestwick in 1860. **(CCU–OBG)**

PARSLOE, George: White Hope of the **Marvis Bay Mafia** in their anti–**Dibble** campaign. Works in the **Cat–Stroker**'s office, is an old friend of **Barbara Medway** and engaged to her greatest chum. When he plays **Ferdinand Dibble** it is with the superior assurance of a man who has, in his time, gone round in ninety–four. **(HOG–THO)**

PATERSON, Alexander: President of the **Paterson Dyeing and Refining Co.**, is a friend of the **Oldest Member**. Has always been a careful rather than a dashing golfer, and adopts a method of preparation which sometimes proves a little exasperating to the highly strung. **(CCU–OBG)**

PATERSON DYEING AND REFINING CO.: short of a treasurer, the post to be won by **Mitchell Holmes** or **Rupert Dixon** following an ordeal by golf. **(CCU–OBG)**

PATIENTS: those yapping weak–mindedly round the new bowling–green. **(HOG–ARP)**

PATMORE, Mabel: flirts disgracefully with **Purvis**, the club Bowls champion. **(HOG–RFQ)**

PATTERNE, Sir Willoughby: another integral part of the character of **Chester Meredith**, as mistakenly assumed by **Felicia Blakeney**. **(HOG–CFO)**

PEABODY, George: in a casual sardine tin in the rough at the eleventh, takes ten; will be lucky if he does a ninety. **(LEO–ALG)**

PEABODY, PEABODY, PEABODY, PEABODY, COOTES, TOOTS AND PEABODY: an old–established legal firm with whom **George Mackintosh** has a good position. **(CCU–SGM)**

PENNEFATHER, George William: heretically states that golf is only a game; merely a pastime. Beaten by **Nathaniel Frisby**, despite receiving a third, he objects to being treated like a leper and being obliquely advised to take up croquet. **(HOG–MPF)**

Barbara Medway asks George Parsloe why tees are called tees

PERFECT PEACE: that peace beyond understanding which comes at its maximum only to the man who has given up golf, visible in the thoughtful and reflective eye of the **Oldest Member**. It is the same expression which, in a lesser degree, you see in the eyes of soldiers home from the wars. Shadrach, Meshach and Abednego had it after they emerged from the fiery furnace; as did Daniel when, with a curt goodbye, he stepped from the lions' den. **(Colliers–OBG)**

PERKINS: a twenty–four–handicap member of the submerged tenth. Playing **Broster** for fifty pounds, missed a two–foot putt on the last by six inches. **(HOG–HST; LEO–ALG)**

PERKINS, George: a sixteen–handicap youth paired with **Marcella Bingley** against **Ramsden Waters** and **Eunice Bray** in the mixed foursomes. Considered an indifferent performer, certain to foozle a few, but at the vital time saw his white ball tumble into the right compartment at roulette. **(CCU–ROS)**

PETTIGREW, Mrs: on recovering a lost purse kissed the **Secretary**'s bald spot, to his observant fiancée Adela's great distress. **(HOG–PRS)**

PHILOSOPHER'S STONE: as sought by alchemists, comparable to **Wallace Chesney**'s search for confidence. **(HOG–MPF)**

PHIPPS, Luella Periton: author of the sizzling Desert Romance *The Love That Scorches*. **(HOG–RFQ)**

PICCADILLY CIRCUS: the **Oldest Member** admires fellows who can plunge into the bowels of the earth at, or at Times Square or Grand Central, and find the right Tube or Subway train with nothing but a lot of misleading signs to guide them. **(CCU–AMT; GWT–AMT; McClure–AMT)**

PICKERING, Harold: a fourteen–handicap player whose love took him down to scratch within a month, before rising to a shaky ten. Fell in love with **Troon (or Merion) Rockett** but after suffering from apparent rejection turned his attention to golf and **Agnes Flack**. **(FQO–SCM; USFQO–SCM)**

PILCHER, Frederick: an eighteen–handicap artist, whose innocent goggling at **Agnes Flack** — to determine her suitability as a model for a series of Felix the Cat–type stories — might have led to disaster. Proved to be a double–crosser of the worst sort, using as his weapons a blob of mud and the eagle eyes of a mastodon of the prehistoric plain. **(MMS–PTT)**

Pirbright under the influence

98

PIRBRIGHT: Celia Todd's Pekinese, whose habit of imbibing tonic port caused him to run up sides of walls and jump from bridges while under the influence. (NSE–TAH)

PIRBRIGHT, Angela: to the surprise and delight of **Walter Judson**, has no insuperable objection to Fiends in human shape, especially if they use the interlocking grip. (FQO–JBW)

PLINLIMMON, Clarice: née **Fitch**, accustomed to quelling charging lions with a glance, trekking untrodden Africa and flying uncharted oceans, so does not take kindly to the unromantic air of a golf club. Mistaken by a glassless Ernest for a sheep, which she subsequently became. (LEO–ALG)

PLINLIMMON, Ernest Faraday: an average–adjuster, not just an average average–adjuster but one who adjusts a beautiful average. The perpetual strain this imposes means he is less skilful than many in the absorption of Portuguese love sonnets. He is no butterfly who flits from flower to flower; average–adjusters are like chartered accountants — when they love, they give their hearts forever. In Ernest's case, to **Clarice**. (LEO–ALG)

PLUS FOURS: the most spectacular, incandescent, pair of which were made to measure by **Cohen Bros.**, second–hand clothiers, for **Sandy McHoots**, who for some reason sent them back. They had for the main *motif* of the fabric a vivid pink, and with this to work on the architect had let his imagination run free, and had produced so much variety in the way of chessboard squares of white, yellow, violet, and green that the eye swam as it looked upon them. The Brothers, or to be accurate, **Lou Cohen**, recognised in **Wallace Chesney** sufficient of the connoisseur to appreciate the beneficial effects to be obtained by playing in apparel of such momentous history.

Under their impact, the adaptability of behaviour of the golf club members was striking. For the first few days they were stunned. Nervous players sent their caddies on in front of them at blind holes, so that they might be warned in time of Wallace's presence ahead and not have him happening to them all of a sudden. And even the Pro was not unaffected. Brought up in Scotland, in an atmosphere of tartan kilts, he nevertheless winced, and a startled "Hoots!" was forced from his lips when Wallace Chesney suddenly appeared in the valley as he was about to drive from the fifth tee. But within about ten days the Plus Fours became a familiar feature of the landscape, and were pointed out to strangers together with the waterfall, the Lover's Leap and the view from the eighth green as things you ought not to miss.

Editorial Comment. According to Geoffrey Jaggard, Lord Lyon King of Arms, the High Commissioner for Scottish Affairs, the Hereditary Lord Keeper of Dunstaffnage Castle and other recognised authorities having been consulted in vain for an identification of the particular Clan tartan here involved, it was his theory that, whilst not, of course, so violent as the tartans of Clan Macmillan or Clan Chattan, there are indications that the designers (Clan Cohen of Covent Garden) may have been confused between the Buchanan sett and that equally picturesque one designed for Her Majesty Queen Victoria known as the Balmoral tartan.

(HOG–MPF)

PLYMOUTH HOE: scene of a tight game of bowls. **(HOG–ARP)**

POBSLEY, Herbert: one of the most pronounced pests of modern civilisation, he talks when on the golf course. **(CCU–SGM)**

PODMARSH, Mrs: wrongly believes her son, **Rollo**, to be a non-smoking teetotaller. **(HOG–ARP)**

PODMARSH, Rollo: only son of a widowed mother, who coddled him since he had been in the nursery with flannel next to the skin, dry shoes and hot arrowroot from September to May inclusive. But he resembles a specimen out of Jack Dempsey's training camp rather than **Mary Kent**'s preconceived vision of a small, slender man with eyebrow moustache and pince–nez. Scores more than a hundred–and–twenty every time (a source of much pride to his mother who is aware that one of the best players in the club, **Mr Burns**, seldom manages to reach eighty), until, when playing with Mary he realises that saying "Oh! Mary! Mary!" or "Ah, Mary!" while driving or using the mashie leads to just the right swing and a good shot. Recognised as a golfing hero because, though he has every reason to suppose himself fatally poisoned, he finishes his round to try to break a hundred for the first time. (HOG–ARP; NSE–FOC)

POE, Edgar Allen (1809–1849): Mabel Somerset would have fitted like the paper on the wall to *The Fall of the House of Usher* by. Ramsden Waters's nurse was the, of her scx. (CCU–SUH,ROS)

PONTO: recently handed in his portfolio after holding office for ten years as the Willoughby family dog. (HOG–ARP)

POO–BOOP–A–DOOP: see teuf–teuf.

POOR PUSSY HOME FOR INDIGENT CATS: on being connected to this, the third successive wrong number, Jane Bates is strongly tempted to apply for admission to it. (HOG–PRS)

POP–EYE: the sailor, compared to Agnes Flack. (NSE–TAH)

POPGOOD & GROOLY: New York publishers of the Book Beautiful. (PLP–SLT.)

POPGOOD, Mr: snr. ptr., Popgood & Grooly. (PLP–SLT)

PORTER, George: against Walter Judson in the final of the President's Cup, played a steady game as befits a teetotal vegetarian. When his engagement was broken, he gave a good impression of having had his insides removed by a taxidermist who had absent–mindedly forgotten to complete the operation by stuffing him. (FQO–JBW)

PORT RICKEY: one of the locations of the wedding of Mortimer Sturgis and Mabel Somerset. The Beach Hotel is recommended. (McClure–SUH)

PORTUGUESE LOVE SONNETS: mandatory reading for prospective suitors. (LEO–ALG)

POSKITT, Gwendoline: beloved of **Wilmot Byng**, and daughter of **Joseph**. She cannot bring herself to forgo the big church wedding with the Bishop doing his stuff and photographs in the shiny weeklies, for she realises that the result of an elopement is that bim would go the Bishop, and phut, the photos. **(LEO–LOL)**

POSKITT, Joseph: unpopularly known to fellow golfers as the **First Gravedigger**, is a member of the **Wrecking Crew**, the golfing quartet of unprecedented incompetence. Has been known to cut the ball in half with his niblick. Was highly fancied to beat **Palsied Percy** for the President's Cup. Got a Blue at Oxford for hammer-throwing not, to **Wilmot Byng**'s surprise, for the high jump. Father of **Gwendoline**, and the d'Artagnan of the links, but with a wife who ruled him with an unremitting firmness from the day they crossed the threshold of **St Peter's, Eaton Square**. **(LEO–LEL)**

POSKITT, Mrs: said "Oh, yeah?" **(LEO–LEL)**

POST, Emily (1872–1960): a ruling by, is equivalent to shooting African chiefs who are under the influence of trade gin. **(NSE–FOC)**

POSTLETHWAITE, Miss: princess of barmaids, at the **Anglers' Rest**. **(MMS–PTT)**

POTTER, Saul: defeated by **B Rockleigh Derrick** in the semi-final of the Rockwell Golf Tournament. **(TEH)**

PREBBLE, Julia: a platinum blonde golfer who, whether through some natural talent for concealing the true merits of her game, or possibly because she is engaged to marry a member of the handicapping committee, contrives to scrounge a twenty-seven handicap for the Ladies' Vase Cup, when ten would have been more than adequate. **(NSE–TAH)**

PRESCOTT, Jack: tricked by **Legs Mortimer** into immobility under water. **(LEO–FTL)**

PRESIDENT'S CUP: classed somewhere between the Grandmother's Umbrella and the All day Sucker competed for by children who have not passed their seventh birthday. **(NSE-EXC)**

PRIG Betsey: her views on Sairey Gamp's friend Mrs Harris coincided with those of **Sally Smith** on **Lottie Higginbotham**. **(DOS)**

PRO, The: finished sixth in the last Open, but had never done the second nine in better than thirty-five at his home course. Accomplished maker of fine, steel-shafted, rubber-grip, self-compensating sets of clubs. In other guises, on other courses, he appears regularly throughout the reminiscences. **(HOG-CFO; LEO-FTL; passim)**

PROMOTER OF THE KING'S HAPPINESS, the: title bestowed on the Scottish missionary, a small, bearded man with bushy eyebrows and face like a walnut brought away in a raid on S'nandrews, who converts the **King of Oom** and his people to the new religion. The title is usually shortened to **The Pro**. **(CCU-COG)**

PROSSER, George: against **Walter Jukes** in the final of the President's Cup, he played the sort of golf King Lear or Hamlet might have played at the height of their troubles. **(JohnBull-KYT)**

PROUST, Marcel (1871-1922): **Smallwood Bessemer** tactlessly advised his fiancée to read. **(Cosmo-IGY)**

PROVIDENCE: by providing a tropical deluge accompanied by thunderbolts, it appeared to **Agnes Flack** that it was at last intervening on behalf of a good woman. **(NSE-FOC)**

PSHAW: **Ralph Bingham** and **Arthur Jukes** were in the mood when men say,. **(CCU-LOH)**

PUBLISHERS: a race of sensitive, highly strung men, whether they be Doubleday, Knopf, Dodd Mead & Co. or the Brothers Harper on the one hand, Knopf, William Morrow, Simon & Schuster, Harper and Charles Scribner's Sons on the other, or even Gollancz, Hamish Hamilton, Chapman & Hall, Heinemann and Herbert Jenkins on the third. **(FQO-SCM, USFQO-SCM, USEGB-SCM)**

PUBLIUS SYRIUS (1st cent BC): one of the first to write an instruction manual for golf, of which, regrettably, only the fragment concerning the backswing remains:

He gets through too late who goes too fast.

(HOG–preface)

PURE REASON: the spirit in which **Vincent Jopp** approached the game of golf. **(CCU–HEA)**

PURITY LEAGUE: jerks *Sewers of the Soul* by **Wilmot Royce** before a tribunal. **(HOG–CFO)**

PURPLE FAN, The: **Rodney Spelvin**'s neo–decadent novel goes through the country like Spanish flu. **(HOG–JGO)**

PURVIS: a golfer who disgraces himself twice — by winning a bowls championship, and then by flirting with **Mabel Patmore**. **(HOG–RFQ)**

PUTTERS: in the brave old days of dudhood, the only p..s you ever found in **Wallace Chesney**'s society were patent self–adjusting things that looked like croquet mallets that had taken the wrong turning in childhood. **(HOG–MPF)**

But according to the **Oldest Member**, the choice of one is so much more important than the choice of a wife. **(CCU–OBG)**

PUTTING STANCES: described by the **Oldest Member** as the Sitting Hen (as practised by **Walter Judson** and **Walter Jukes**), the Paralytic (or Paralytic Crouch), and the Lumbago Stoop (or Lumbago Crouch). **(FQO–JBW; JohnBull–KYT)**

PYTHIAS: **Damon** and, compare to **Peter Willard** and **James Todd**. **(CCU–WOW)**

QUEEN'S HALL: before **Wood Hills** on **Brusiloff**'s itinerary. **(CCU–COC)**

QUICK RESULTS AGENCY: a private inquiry concern which, among other blessings, bestows detectives disguised as caddies upon golfers who nurse unworthy suspicions of their opponents. **(HOG–HST)**

QUILL, Colonel: took up golf at the age of fifty–six, and by devising an ingenious machine, consisting of a fishing–line and sawn–down bedpost, was enabled to keep his head so still he became a scratch player within a year. **(CCU–HEA)**

RAMAGE: passing through a trying time, a dumb Isaac watching **Mabel Patmore** flirt with **Purvis**. **(HOG–RFQ)**

RAVIOGLI, Princessa della: saved from the Indian Ocean by **Captain Jack Fosdyke**, despite half a dozen sharks getting in the way and hampering him, horsing about and behaving as if the place belonged to them. **(NSE–FOC)**

RAY, Ted: mentioned the tendency to snatch back the club. Smokes all the time he's playing. Author of *Taking Turf*. **(HOG–THG,ARP; CCU–SGM)**

REAL GOLF: a thing of the spirit, not of mere technical excellence of stroke. **(CCU–WOW)**

ROBERTSON, Robert: see **John Henrie**. **(CCU)**

ROBINSON: wins a golf match against the redoubtable **Angus McTavish** by a hole — in the Scotsman's trouser pocket. **(CCU–HEA)**

ROCKETT: a familiar but highly confusing family. John, the famous father, was reported to have twice won the British Amateur Championship and three times been runner–up in the Open. But elsewhere he is credited instead with being three times the US and twice the British Amateur Champion, or even twice the (US) Amateur Champion and three times the (US) Open runner–up. Long since retired from competition golf, the great veteran is engaged in his reminiscences and living in leisured ease with his family — his grandmother, now ageing a little but in her day a demon with the gutty ball; his wife, at one time British Ladies' Champion and Woman Champion of America; and his children. It is here that the confused reporting about the family gives greatest cause for concern. Their biographer is not able accurately to determine whether the alternative names credited to the five were merely the result of their temporary whims, or to meet the sensitivities of the local residents of the UK and US from time to time, or whether they were actually christened with all these names. Or even whether there were indeed twelve Rockett children, though that does seem unlikely on the evidence.

One thing seems certain — that the children were named after the courses on which he won renown. His three sons were Sandwich, Hoylake and St Andrew, or Pinehurst, Baltusrol and Winged Foot, or yet again, National, Baltusrol and Wykagyl; his daughters, more simply, are known either as Troon and Prestwick, or Minikhada and Merion. Whichever selection is preferred, it can be said with confidence that they have not yet disgraced their honoured names — all have become scratch, although Troon/Merion is very comfortable at the prospect of marrying a ten–handicap man in the shape of **Harold Pickering**, and allowing her own game to drift to his level. **(FQO–SCM; USFQO–SCM; USEGB–SCM; Strand–TFT)**

ROCKING HORSE: the catalyst for a change in **Sally Smith**'s attitude to **Bill Paradene**, when she imagines him sitting on it with his little fat legs hanging down. So taken is she with the transformation that she attributes to it magical powers, and despite its lack of wings they agree that one can fly on it to a world which is clean and simple. **(GOO)**

ROCKY MOUNTAINS: home of grizzly bears, to be shot by **Ambrose Gussett**. **(NSE–UFD)**

ROGIE, Pat: see **John Henrie**. **(CCU)**

ROLLER SKATES: the cause of a moving experience for **Angus McTavish**. **(LEO–FTL)**

ROLLITT, Professor Orlando (or Dwight Z): swipes some of the **Emperor Marcus Aurelius's** best stuff for his book *Are You Your Own Master?*, the copyright having expired some 2,000 years earlier. **(CCU–OBG; Colliers–OBG)**

ROMAN EMPERORS, the later: the insane arrogance of, emerged because they had never played golf. **(HOG–MPF)**

ROYCE, Wilmot: mother of **Felicia Blakeney** and novelist, whose last work, *Sewers of the Soul*, was jerked before a tribunal by the **Purity League**. Also wrote *The Stench of Life* and *Grey Mildew* (and its companion, *Gray Mildew*) **(HOG–CFO; SatEvePost–CFO)**

R P CRUMBLES, INC.: purveyors of Silver Sardines (the Sardine with a Soul), and employer of **Harold Bewstridge**. **(NSE–EXC)**

RUBBO: specific used by **Agnes Flack**, but frowned on by **Smallwood Bessemer**. **(Cosmo–IGY)**

RULE 853: a golf–lawyer proves, by section two sub–section four of, that you've disqualified yourself by having an ingrowing toenail. **(CCU–LOH)**

SAGE, the: see **Oldest Member**.

ST. BRULE: **Mortimer Sturgis** married **Mabel Somerset** quietly at, instead of the florid ceremony he had planned at St. George's, Hanover Square. **(CCU–SUH)**

ST. PETER'S, EATON SQUARE: scene of the nuptials of **Wilmot Byng** and **Gwendoline Poskitt**, when, we are informed, it was generally agreed that the vicar had never been in better voice. **(LEO–LOL)**

SALVINI, Tommaso (1830–1915): the manner of the great tragedian in the pillow scene in **Othello** resembled that of **William Bates**. **(HOG–PRS)**

SAMUEL, the infant, in prayer: statuette of, broken by **Mortimer Sturgis**. **(CCU–SUH)**

SAN FRANCISCO EARTHQUAKE: insignificant compared to **Lottie Higginbotham**'s reaction when told her new hat looked like nothing on earth. **(DOS)**

SARAZEN, Gene: partnered **Cuthbert Banks**. **(GWT–COC)**

SARDINE OPENER: **Jack Fosdyke** claims to have once killed a lion with a. **(NSE–FOC)**

SCHLOSSING–LOSSING, Prince of: amused by Legs. **(LEO–FTL)**

SCOTCH BLOOD: makes for solid worth rather than nimbleness of wit, and for a certain rugged stability of character rather than quick intuition. **(LEO–FTL)**

SCOTSMAN, a: to be, a hard thing to say of anyone. **(CCU–COG)**

"Have you ever seen a happy pro?"

"No. I don't think I have.... But pros are all Scotchmen."

(HOG–THG)

SCRUBS, Wormwood: home from home for black–souled golfers. **(CCU–OBG)**

SEAWEED: **Eunice Bray**'s aunt collected dried, as a hobby, and pasted it in an album. One sometimes thinks that aunts live entirely for pleasure. **(CCU–ROS)**

SECRETARY, the: of the Club, courteous and efficient, when not looking for *The Man with the Missing Eyeball*, is concerned about the civility of **Ramage**. But his spotless reputation is tarnished when, in an example of the liberty of a free country degenerating into licence, he occupies the **Oldest Member**'s favourite chair. (**HOG-RFQ,JGO,PRS**)

SEPTEMBER 7: forgotten each year by **William Bates**. (**HOG-JGO**)

SEX MOTIF: its absence from **Prof Farmer**'s *Sleepy Time* causes **Cyril Grooly** to decide to restrict his offer of advance royalties to $ 100. (**PLP-SLT**)

SHADRACH, MESHACH and ABEDNEGO: Smallwood Bessemer felt like. (**NSE-TAH**)

SHAKESPEARE, William (1564-1616): wrote a sketch for the **Wrecking Crew**, in which, recognising their tendency to hold up impatient foursomes behind, he gave one of them the apposite line:

Four rogues in buckram let drive at me.

(**HOG-Preface**)

SIGSBEE: a **Cape Pleasanter**, who lost to **Mealing**. (**MUP-ARB**)

SIMPSON, Jane: is given a formula for knitting jumpers. (**HOG-ARP**)

SINGER BUILDING : not used by **Celia Tennant** to hit **George Mackintosh** — it was only a niblick. (**McClure-SGM**)

SINGER'S MIDGET TROUPE: tended to link their lot with women of five foot eleven. (**NSE-FOC**)

SING SING: where **Bradbury Fisher** and **J Gladstone Bott** pursued their intense rivalry, Fisher securing the position of catcher on the baseball nine and getting the last place on the crossword puzzle team, while Bott was chosen as tenor for the glee club and was selected for the debating club. (**HOG-HST**)

SLYTHE & SAYLE, Lord: witness to **Jack Fosdyke**'s adroitness. (**NSE-FOC**)

SMETHURST, Adeline: could not have gazed at **Raymond Devine** more rapturously if he had been a saucer of ice–cream. Until, of course, his exposure for what he was by **Vladimir Brusiloff**, following which she began to appreciate **Cuthbert Banks**'s sincerity in his belief that she stood out from the company like a jewel in a pile of coke, and that she made the rest look like battered repaints.

According to the late Henry Longhurst, in his essay *That Varied Never–Ending Pageant that Men Call Golf* in *Homage to P G Wodehouse* (1973, Barrie & Jenkins), the reference to 'battered repaints' is to the habit in the early years of the twentieth century of repainting an old golf ball by rolling it in a film of white paint in the palms, and laying it out to dry on a board of upturned nails. **(CCU–COC)**

SMETHURST, Mrs Willoughby: president of **Wood Hills Literary and Debating Society**, and tripler of its membership. Her unfaltering resolve was that never while she had her strength should the soul be handed the loser's end. **Adeline**'s aunt. **(CCU–COC)**

SMITH, Dr Sally: res. 61 Alderney St, S W. Small, pretty, and extraordinarily capable with the mashie. An American who learned her golf at Garden City, New York, where her handicap is six. Devoted to the work ethic, she has no time for loafers, although she will let them prod her legs and perversely encourages them to ride rocking–horses. Dares not say "Good Morning" too often. **(DOS; GOO)**

SMITHERS: a refined and dyeing man, about to retire. **(CCU–OBG)**

SMITHSON, Dr: proposed by the **Oldest Member** as a suitable companion for **Mortimer Sturgis** in the game of ball–hunting in the club–house. **(CCU–AMT)**

The Catalyst

111

Mabel Somerset returns to her husband

112

SMOKING: according to **Mrs Podmarsh,** causes nervous dyspepsia, sleeplessness, gnawing of the stomach, headache, weak eyes, red spots on the skin, throat irritation, asthma, bronchitis, heart failure, lung trouble, catarrh, melancholy, neurasthenia, loss of memory, impaired will–power, rheumatism, lumbago, sciatica, neuritis, heartburn, torpid liver, loss of appetite, enervation, lassitude, lack of ambition and falling out of hair. **(HOG–ARP)**

SNAKES: Harold Pickering would have challenged the charge that they steal girls' hearts behind people's backs, if he had had the opportunity. **(FQO–SCM)**

SNEEZO: the Sovereign Remedy lowered in pailsful in the Rabbits' Umbrella by **Joe Stocker.** But it loses its power to protect when confronted by a direct frontal attack in the form of a nosegay of flowers. **(NSE–RHR)**

SOCRATES (c470–399BC): a Greek Bozo, whose name when abbreviated to Socks or Sox was expected to calm **Walter Judson** or **Walter Jukes** down. **(FQO–JBW; JohnBull–KYT)**

SOMERSET, Mabel: not **Mary**; a fragile–looking girl with big blue eyes, a cloud of golden hair, a sweet expression and a left wrist in a sling. To watch her holing out her soup gave **Mortimer Sturgis** a sort of feeling you get when your drive collides with a rock in the middle of a tangle of rough and kicks back into the middle of the fairway. Ladies' Open Croquet Champion. **(CCU–SUH)**

SOMERSET, Mary: the winner of the Ladies' Open, but not **Mrs Mortimer Sturgis. (CCU–SUH)**

SOUND VIEW GOLF CLUB: close to Great Neck, where Wodehouse lived in the period from about 1918 to 1920, and where he obtained the ideas for most of the **Oldest Member** stories. According to David Jasen in *A Portrait of a Master* (1975, Garnstone Press Ltd), it was infested with actors — including Roy Barnes, Donald Brain, Ernest Truex and Ed Wynn — with whom Wodehouse would play golf, though he was not any good at it.

SOVIETSKI: the eminent contemporary Russian novelist, is spitted of. Influenced **Devine** to his ultimate infinite distress. The law could not touch you for being influenced but there is an ethical as well as a legal code. **(CCU–COC)**

SPEECH, gift of: that which places Man in a class of his own, above the ox, the ass, the common wart–hog, and the rest of the lower animals. **(MLF–WIH)**

SPELVIN, Anastasia: née **Bates**, sister of **William**, and a scratch golfer. On the putting–green of Anastasia's marital happiness, however, there lurks a secret worm–cast. **(HOG–PRS; NSE–RHR)**

SPELVIN, George: actor cousin of **Rodney**, with histrionic ambitions. **(HOG–RFQ)**

SPELVIN, Rodney: tall, slim, dark, sickeningly romantic–looking youth in faultless serge, formerly a fairly virulent poet who would produce a slim volume of verse bound in squashy mauve leather at the drop of a hat, mostly containing illusions about pixies and descriptions of sunsets. Signed up **Anastasia Bates** for life's medal round after numerous flirtations including more than one with **Jane Packard,** during which with zealous hand he brushed ants off her mayonnaise and squashed wasps with a chivalrous teaspoon. Five years later, was shown to have forgotten her completely. **William Bates** thought he should have been lynched years ago, and suggests that it looks like negligence that he was not. Jane seems to agree when she looks at him as at a caterpillar in a salad. Is now a stalwart golfer with occasional lapses, during one of which, though he reverts to his poetic mode, it is in a different style, the school of Christopher Robin. **(HOG–RFQ,JGO,PRS; NSE–RHR)**

SPELVIN, Timothy: offspring of **Rodney** and **Anastasia,** exploited by his lapsing father as **Timothy Bobbin** in several ghastly poems in a rare satirical attack by Wodehouse on a fellow artist, A A Milne, who had been very publicly uncharitable. Under his father's influence, he hammed up every situation, using bluebells, in their secondary role as fairy telephones, to call up Fairy Queens to invite them to his teddy bear's birthday party. **(NSE–RHR)**

Rodney Spelvin demonstrates his technique with the spoons

115

Timothy Bobbin

SPENLOW, Rowland: into whose soul remorse bit like an adder. (HOG–JGO)

SPOTTSWORTH, Cora McGuffy: a pre–Raphaelite disciple whose publisher's slogan is *Spottsworth for Blushes* and who looks like one of those women who lure men's souls to the shoals of sin. Attaching herself like a limpet to the notable golfer **Sidney McMurdo**, she all but cuts out **Agnes Flack**, that Diana of the links. It might be that she would at some future date put arsenic in his coffee or elope with the leader of a band, but before she did so, she would in all essential respects be a worthy mate. She might, and probably would, recline on tiger skins in the nude and expect Sidney to drink champagne out of her shoe, but she would never wear high heels on the links or say "Tee–hee" when she missed a putt. (**NSE–FOC**)

SPOTTSWORTH, Mr: a low hound who has left **Cora** through double pneumonia, probably reincarnated as a jelly–fish. (**NSE–FOC**)

SPROCKETT, Lulabelle: the heiress of Sprockett's Superfine Sardines is worth a hundred million dollars in her own right, but can even wealth on this scale excuse her for referring to golf as hockey–knocking? (**NSE–FOC**)

SQUASHY HOLLOW GOLF CLUB: An apparently popular name for golf courses, appearing as it clearly does on both sides of the Atlantic and, in the case of the USA, in at least two different locations. The first of these is five miles from Goldenville, Long Island, where **Bradbury Fisher** won his first competition (**HOG–KIW**). The second is near Paradise Valley, and benefits from soft mountain breezes (**PLP–SLT**). An English course of this name appears in **HOG–RFQ** and **PRS**, and is also mentioned in the story *Portrait of a Disciplinarian*, in *Meet Mr Mulliner*.

Be that as it may, **Agnes Flack** does the third hole in one at, and it would seem likely that the course where this was achieved was in the United States. (**NSE–FOC**)

William Bates defers proposing to **Jane Packard** to compete in the Invitation Tournament at the English course. (**HOG–RFQ**)

117

The course near Paradise Valley is the scene of **McMurdo** v **Grooly** and, although in the USA, had been constructed by an exiled Scot who modelled the eighteen holes on the nastiest and most repellent of his native land, such as the Sahara at Sandwich, the Alps at Prestwick, the Stationmaster's Garden at St Andrew's, the Eden and the Redan. And as the description of this course equates precisely with that describing the National links at Southampton, Long Island, in the Preface to *The Heart of a Goof*, who is to say that the Paradise Valley Squashy Hollow is not the authentic version, all the others merely being Hollow substitutes?

STICKO: the pomade that satisfies. **(NSE–FOC)**

STOCKER, Joseph: a muscle–bound golfer, suffering from hay–fever, performs prodigies in the final round of the Rabbits' Umbrella against **Rodney Spelvin**. Capable of breaking large vases with his paroxysms, making them fly across the room and be dashed to pieces against the wall. But susceptible to the influence of **Sneezo**. A famous amateur wrestler in his youth, he made up for what he lacked in finesse by bringing to the links the rugged strength and directness of purpose which in other days had enabled him to pin one and all to the mat: and it had been well said of him that as a golfer you never knew what he was going to do next. He has been known to do the long fifteenth in two, and the short second in thirty–seven. In the final he made history immediately by holing out his opening drive. It is true that he holed it out on the sixteenth green, which lies some three hundred yards away and a good deal to the left of the first tee, but he holed it out, and a gasp went up from the spectators. If this was what Joseph Stocker did on the first, they said to one another, the imagination reeled stunned at the prospect of the heights to which he might soar in the course of eighteen holes. **(NSE–RHR)**

STURGIS, Mortimer: a carefree 38–year old of independent means, with an amiable character, a creditable ability at tennis, a baritone voice sufficient to perform solos at charity concerts, no serious vices other than the collecting of porcelain vases, a charming fiancée in **Betty Weston** and a desire for secret golf lessons. When he was stymied in life's medal round by Betty's withdrawal from the running, he turned by mistake to croquet champion **Mabel Somerset**, and

Joseph Stocker's allergy

declared that he would rather call her "Mary" than do the first hole at Muirfield (or, as the case may be, at the Engineers' Club at Rosslyn) in two. **(CCU-AMT,SUH)**

STURGISes, sundry: fantasy figments of **Mortimer**'s imagination included Harry Vardon Sturgis, J H Taylor Sturgis, George Duncan Sturgis, Abe Mitchell Sturgis, Harold Hilton Sturgis, Edward Ray Sturgis, Horace Hutchinson Sturgis and James Braid Sturgis. **(CCU-AMT)**

> "Weren't you going to have rather a large family?"
>
> "Was I? I don't know. What's bogey?"

Presumably today, one would ask instead, "Who's par?" **(CCU-AMT)**

We should not overlook his potential American family either, consisting of Walter Hagen Sturgis, Chick Evans Sturgis, Francis Ouimet Sturgis, James Barnes Sturgis, Jerome Travers Sturgis, Mike Brady Sturgis, John Hutchinson Sturgis and George McLean Sturgis. **(McClure-AMT)**

SWAN: and **Edgar**, compare to **Peter Willard** and **James Todd**. **(CCU-WOW)**

SYBARITES' CLUB: where **Cape Pleasant** members tend to meet. **(MUP-ARB)**

TAGORE, Sir Rabinadrath (1861-1941): never tried a T-bone in his life. **(NSE-RHR)**

TAJ MAHAL: a pretty nifty tomb. **(CCU-COC)**

TAYLOR, John Henry: warned against dropping the right shoulder. Skilled at hitting balls cleanly out of indentations in the turf. Advises putting off the right leg. Former owner of a shirt stud which finds its way into **Bradbury Fisher**'s collection. Author of *On the Chip Shot* and *On The Push Shot* (**HOG–THG, HST; CCU–SUH, ROS; Colliers–OBG; DOS; GOO**)

TEE:

> "Do you like a high tee?" he asked.

> "Oh, no," she replied. "Doctors say it's indigestible."

(McClure–SUH)

TENNANT, Celia: fears that her fiancé, when called upon to reply "I will", is liable to go up into the pulpit and deliver an address on *Marriage Customs Through the Ages*. Solves the problem of **Gabby George Mackintosh** in a practical way by attempting to murder him with a niblick. (**CCU–SGM**)

TENNIS PRO: astounded by the revelation that there are other games. (**NSE–UFD**)

TEUF–TEUF: see **tinkerty–tonk**.

TEWKESBURY, Evangeline: in the eyes of her male acquaintance is just what the doctor ordered and, in the event, is just what the doctor got. For though a mere tennis player, temporarily confused by the belief that golf is a footling game for the half-witted, before achieving a painstaking eighteen handicap, she is honoured by a proposal of marriage from that notable scratch performer **Dr Ambrose Gussett**, the psittacine expert. (**NSE–UFD**)

TEWKESBURY, Martha: informative aunt of the lass who loves and weds above her station, providing the key to the loved one's medicine box. (**NSE–UFD**)

121

THOSE IN PERIL ON THE TEE

The story of this title appeared in the magazines some two years before it was included in the collection **Mr Mulliner Speaking** *in both the UK and the US. During this period it evolved from an Oldest Member story into a Mulliner tale, and the distant relationship between the Mulliner clan and Agnes Flack was introduced.*

It was a morning when all nature shouted "Fore!" **(HOG–THG)**

* * *

I had often seen the Wrecking Crew, that quartette of spavined septuagenarians whose pride it was that they never let anyone through, scatter like leaves in an autumn gale at the sound of Agnes Flack's stentorian "Fore!" **(FQO–SCM)**

* * *

It is estimated that there are twenty–three important points to be borne in mind simultaneously while making a drive at golf; and to the man who has mastered the art of remembering them all the task of hiding girls in taxi–cabs is mere child's play.

"Thank you so much," murmured a voice behind him. It seemed to come from the floor.

"Not at all," said George, trying a sort of vocal chip–shot out of the corner of his mouth, designed to lift his voice backwards and lay it dead inside the cab. **(ADD)**

* * *

122

"Cora expects to win the Women's Singles", said Sidney.

Agnes drew herself up haughtily. She was expecting to win the Women's Singles herself.

"She does, does she?"

"Yes, she does."

"Over my dead body."

"That would be a mashie niblick shot," said Sidney McMurdo thoughtfully.   (NSE–FOC)

* * *

His ball was entangled in a bush of considerable size, from which it seemed that it could be removed only with a pair of tweezers. ...... It was at moments like this that you caught Joseph Stocker at his best. ...... When it came to a straight issue of muscle and the will to win, he stood alone. Here was where he could use his niblick, and Joe Stocker, armed with his niblick, was like King Arthur wielding his sword Excalibur. The next instant, the ball, the bush, a last year's bird's nest and a family of caterpillars which had taken out squatters' rights were hurtling through the air towards the green. (NSE–RHR)

* * *

Friend calls out to a beginner, "How are you getting on, old man?" and the beginner says, "Splendidly. I just made three perfect putts on the last green!" (CCU–OBG)

* * *

Alexander Paterson has always been a careful rather than a dashing player. It is his custom, a sort of ritual, to take two measured practice swings before addressing the ball, even on the putting–green. When he does address the ball he shuffles his feet for a moment or two, then pauses, and scans the horizon in a suspicious sort of way, as if he had been expecting it to play some sort of trick on him when he was not looking. A careful inspection seems to convince him of the horizon's *bona fides,* and he turns his attention to the ball again. He shuffles his feet once more, then raises his club. He waggles the club smartly over the ball three times, then lays it behind the globule. At this point he suddenly peers at the horizon again, in the apparent hope of catching it off its guard. This done, he raises the club very slowly, brings it back very slowly till it almost touches the ball, raises it again, brings it down again, raises it once more, and brings it down for the third time. He then stands motionless, wrapped in thought, like some Indian fakir contemplating the infinite. Then he raises the club again and replaces it behind the ball. Finally he quivers all over, swings very slowly back, and drives the ball for about a hundred and fifty yards in a dead straight line.

It is a method of procedure which sometimes proves a little exasperating to the highly strung. (CCU–OBG)

* * *

"Gedge!" Senator Opal uttered a short, barking sound. "I've no use for Gedge. A fellow who says he had a five on the ninth, and I saw him with my own eyes take four niblick shots in the gully."

Packy found himself warming to this Gedge. A man who could attempt to chisel Senator Opal in a golf game must have striking qualities of enterprise and determination. (HOW)

* * *

His drive had not been anything to write to the golfing journals about, but he was picking up the technique of the game.

"What happened then?"

I told him in a word.

"Your stance was wrong, and your grip was wrong, and you moved your head, and swayed your body, and took your eye off the ball, and pressed, and forgot to use your wrists, and swung back too fast, and let the hands get ahead of the club, and lost your balance, and omitted to pivot on the ball of the left foot, and bent your right knee."

He was silent for a moment.

"There is more to this pastime," he said, "than the casual observer would suspect." **(CCU–AMT)**

* * *

Few crises, however unexpected, have the power to disturb a man who has conquered the weakness of the flesh as to have trained himself to bend his left knee, raise his left heel, swing his arms well out from the body, twist himself into the shape of a corkscrew and use the muscle of the wrist, at the same time keeping his head still and his eye on the ball. **(ADD)**

* * *

Every night before he went to bed he would read the golden words of some master on the subject of putting, driving or approaching. Yet on the links most of his time was spent in retrieving lost balls or replacing America. **(MUP–ARB)**

* * *

125

"You have broken off the engagement?"

"Not exactly. And yet — well, I suppose it amounts to that."

"I don't quite understand."

"Well the fact is," said Celia, in a burst of girlish frankness, "I rather think I've killed George."

"Killed him, eh?"

It was a solution that had not occurred to me, but now that it was presented for my inspection I could see its merits. In these days of national effort, when we are all working together to try to make our beloved land fit for heroes to live in, it was astonishing that nobody had thought of a simple, obvious thing like killing George Mackintosh. George Mackintosh was undoubtedly better dead, but it had taken a woman's intuition to see it.

"I killed him with my niblick," said Celia.

I nodded. If the thing was to be done at all, it was unquestionably a niblick shot. **(CCU–SGM)**

* * *

That warm–hearted, enthusiastic girl, all eagerness to see the man she loves do well — Archie, poor old Archie, all on fire to prove to her that her trust in him is not misplaced, and the end — Disillusionment — Disappointment — Unhappiness. **(MUP–ARB)**

* * *

"Just to think of taking three putts on a green. It will be heaven." **(FQO–SCM)**

* * *

126

Even as her driver rose above her shoulder she was acutely aware that she was making eighteen out of the twenty-three errors which complicate the drive at golf. She knew that her head had swayed like some beautiful flower in a stiff breeze. The heel of her left foot was pointing down the course. Her grip had shifted, and her wrists felt like sticks of boiled asparagus. As the club began to descend she perceived that she had underestimated the total of her errors. And when the ball, badly topped, bounded down the slope and entered the muddy water like a timid diver on a cold morning she realised that she had a full hand. There are twenty-three things which it is possible to do wrong in the drive, and she had done them all. **(CCU-ROS)**

* * *

Everyone who has seen Archibald Mealing play golf knows that his teeing off is one of the most impressive sights ever witnessed on the links. He tilted his cap over his eyes, waggled his club a little, shifted his feet, waggled his club some more, gazed keenly towards the horizon for a moment, waggled his club again, and finally, with the air of a Strong Man lifting a bar of iron, raised it slowly above his head. Then, bringing it down with a sweep, he drove the ball with a lofty slice some fifty yards. It was rarely that he failed either to slice or pull his ball. His progress from hole to hole was generally a majestic zigzag. **(MUP-ARB)**

* * *

This made him two up and three to play. What the average golfer would consider a commanding lead. But Archibald was no average golfer. A commanding lead for him would have been two up and one to play. **(MUP-ARB)**

* * *

127

"You can't move that dog," she said. "It's a hazard."

"Nonsense."

"I beg your pardon, it is. If you get into casual water, you don't mop it up with a brush and pail, do you? Certainly you don't. You play out of it. Same thing when you get into a casual dog." **(NSE–FOC)**

* * *

Beads of perspiration stood out on Mr Derrick's forehead. His play became wilder and wilder at each hole in arithmetical progression. If he had been a plow, he could hardly have turned up more soil. **(Vanfair–TEH)**

* * *

He called up Agnes Flack.

"Miss Flack?"

"Hello?"

"Sorry to disturb you at this hour, but will you marry me?"

"Certainly. Who is that?"

"Smallwood Bessemer."

"I don't get the second name."

"Bessemer. B for banana, e for erysipelas –"

"Oh, Bessemer? Yes, delighted. Good night, Mr Bessemer."

"Good night, Miss Flack." **(NSE–TAH)**

* * *

128

A feeling of calm and content stole over William. He was not sorry for Mr Derrick. Once, when the latter missed the ball clean at the tee, their eyes met, but William saved his life by not smiling. **(Vanfair–TEH)**

* * *

....Poskitt coughed.

I have heard much coughing in my time. I am a regular theatre–goer, and I was once at a luncheon where an operatic basso got a crumb in the windpipe. But never have I heard a cough so stupendous as that which Joseph Poskitt emitted at this juncture. It was as if he had put a strong man's whole soul into the thing. **(LEO–LEL)**

* * *

"If I didn't hook, I sliced. And if I didn't slice I topped."

"That's too bad."

"I only needed a nine to win the fourteenth and I ought to have got it easily. But I blew up on the green."

"That's often the way, isn't it?" **(DOS)**

* * *

Here was the only girl he had ever really loved, and he had no sooner left her than she started holding hands with a man of advanced years in a suit of plus fours of the kind that makes horses shy. He cleared his throat austerely, and was about to speak when the plus–foured one turned.

If one of the more austere of the minor prophets had worn plus fours he would have looked just as Sir Hugo Drake was looking now. **(DOS)**

129

TIDMOUTH, Lord: formerly **Bixby**, and still known as Squiffy. Monocled and bespatted, friend of **Bill Paradene/Bannister**, whose hobbies seem to be getting married and recovering lost umbrellas. Has four recorded wives, though denies the first in **GOO**, presumably because it was before he came into the title. They had the following varied backgrounds:

Mrs Bixby the first	Lottie Burke, a Balham Burke
Lady Tidmouth the first	A half–Spanish lady, who ran away with a Frenchman
Lady Tidmouth the second	A lady who ran away with a Spaniard
Lady Tidmouth the third	A lady who ran away with a Brazilian

And there seems to be general agreement that **Lottie Burke/Higginbotham** will come back into the picture as the fourth Lady Tidmouth. **(DOS; GOO)**

TILFORD: who now can explain why **Park** was attracted to? **(GWT–WOW)**

TINKERTY–TONK: see **toodle–oo**.

TINKY–TING: the Pekingese belonging to **Luella Mainprice Jopp** which helps to unstring **Vincent Jopp**. **(CCU–HEA)**

TODD, Celia: one of the four souls who, speaking even conservatively, pass through the furnace. Described by **Sidney McMurdo** during their brief engagement as a frightful pie–faced little squirt. But then he was unmistakeably large. **(NSE–TAH)**

TODD, James: small and slender, his advocates claim that no one has surpassed him in absolute incompetence with the spoon. **(CCU–WOW)**

TOLSTOI, Count Leo Nikolayevitch (1828–1910): not bad. Not good, but not bad. **(CCU–COC)**

TOODLE–OO: one of many expressions which can be translated as "Good–bye", and used by **Lord Tidmouth. (DOS)**

TOOTING, Vicar of: S.W., is a scratch golfer, excelling at short approach shots, and recommending *The Voice that Breathed O'er St Andrews* as a wedding song. **(CCU–SUH)**

In his contribution to *Homage to P. G. Wodehouse* (Barrie & Jenkins, 1973), the late Henry Longhurst pointed out that the Tooting Bec golf club had been founded on Tooting Common, in the heart of suburban London, in 1888, with the Rt Hon A J Balfour (a future Prime Minister) as President. It was included in Horace Hutchinson's *British Golf Links* and in 1891 became the first home of the Parliamentary Golf Handicap. "Only players who use their iron deftly," wrote Hutchinson, "can expect to get round in under three figures."

TRAVIS, Walter J: nearly forty before he touched a club, but later won the British Amateur. His lofting shot was the cause of a broken mirror. **(HOG–PRS; MUP–ARB)**

TRIED IN THE FURNACE: a film in which **Gloria Gooch** goes by night to the apartment of the libertine, to beg him to spare her sister, whom he has entangled in his toils. **(HOG–PRS)**

TRIVETT, Amanda: the prize in the golf match over the sixteen miles of the world's longest hole. But her secret engagement to the phantom golfer of Little–Mudbury–in–the–Wold leads to disappointment in two breasts and the sale of one new mashie-niblick. Renamed **Amelia** in **GWT–LOH. (CCU–LOH)**

TROTSKY, Leon (Lev Davidovitch Bronstein) (1879–1940): plays with **Lenin** in a foursome at **Nijni Novgorod. (CCU–COC)**

TRUMAN, Harry (1884–1972): lunch partner of **Jack Fosdyke**. (NSE–FOC)

TUSCAN HILLS, the: viewing them from a point on the Torre Rose, Fiesole (or Fuesole, as the UK first edition of **CCU** (Herbert Jenkins) and the US first edition of **DIV** (Doran) prefer), **Mortimer Sturgis** considers them a nasty bit of rough which would take a deal of getting out of. It is **Strand** magazine which first gets it right. (CCU–SUH)

TUTTLE, Mr: Barbara Medway's mother's brother, a lawyer and Cat-stroker; a veteran golfer at **Marvis Bay**, evolves a plan for taking **Ferdinand Dibble** down a peg or two. (HOG–THG)

TWENTIETH CENTURY LIMITED: could have been stopped by **George Mackintosh** on its way to Chicago. (GWT–SGM)

UMBRELLA: a necessary accessory to a honeymoon, as demonstrated three times already by **Lord Tidmouth**, whose unconscious belief in its powers is so strong that, despite his record of losing wives at regular intervals, he still has it with him as he sets out on the path leading to number four. And it isn't even his! (GOO)

UNFORTUNATE INCIDENTS: a class of member of which **Peter Willard** was the best example. (HOG–MPF)

VADUN: a prophet of **Oom**. (CCU–COG)

VANSTONE, Ermyntrude: suffered violently in chapter forty–one of *Grey Eyes That Gleam*. (CCU–ROS)

VARDEN, Dolly: not **Harry**. (CCU–SUH)

VARDON, Harry: swung back smoothly, inveighed against any movement of the head. His books had animated illustrations. Author of *Vardon on Casual Water, Complete Golfer, On the Swing* and *What Every Young Golfer Should Know*. (HOG–THG, HST,MPF,ARP,RFQ; Colliers–OBG; CCU–ROS)

VENUS: brushing flies off a sleeping, is compared to the care shown by **Archibald Mealing** when putting at the thirteenth. **(MUP–ARB)**

VESPASIAN, Temple of: Mortimer Sturgis thought it would be a devil of a place to be bunkered behind. **(CCU–SUH)**

VIENNA BON–TON BAKERY: where they bake a custard–pie that might be **Rodney Spelvin**'s brother. **(HOG–JGO)**

VILLAGE BLACKSMITH: like **Sally Smith**, owes not any man. **(GOO)**

VIOLETS, White: to be sent to **Jane Packard** by **William Bates** on their anniversary each year, and to be misinterpreted. **(HOG–JGO)**

VOLGA BOATMAN: normally has face drawn, manner listless, but if he learned that Stalin had purged his employer he would have gleaming eyes and set lips instead. **(NSE–EXC)**

VOLTERRAGIN and VEENER SIRADZEN: it gives **Vladimir Brusiloff** the pipovitch that he has not met, while touring America. **(GWT–COC)**

VOSPER, Hildebrand: butler to his Grace the Duke of Bootle for eighteen years, until he decides he can no longer stand the sight of the back of his head, and falls easy prey to a determined **Evangeline Fisher**. He becomes the star turn of her Californian ménage, where he is considered immeasurably superior to his predecessor, **Blizzard**. He has to be humoured to prevent **Evangeline** from divorcing **Bradbury Fisher**. **(HOG–HST,KIW)**

WALKER CUP: to the team for which **Sidney McMurdo** would give added strength. **(FQO–SCM)**

WALPURGIS NIGHT: President's Cup day, when fearful things are abroad and the prudent golfer stays at home, resembles. **(LEO–LEL)**

WAPSHOTT–ON–THE–WAP: Hants family seat of **Jack Fosdyke**, at Wapshott Castle. **(NSE–FOC)**

WASPS: do not bite, according to **Wadsworth Hemmingway**. **(LEO–LEL)**

WATERFIELD, Jane: at school with **Felicia Blakeney**. **(HOG–CFO)**

WATERS, Ramsden: with pale saffron hair, a receding forehead, pale blue eyes, and a mouth with a pale, weak smile, from the centre of which protruded two teeth of rabbit–like character, he had apparently been blessed with a shrinking nature from earliest youth, and as much ferocity and self–assertion as a blancmange. But a rugged Viking in private, with a twitchy foot, to boot. **(CCU–ROS)**

WATSON, Betty: see **Betty Weston**, who seems to have changed her name to **Watson** in McIlvaine A27a14, the Penguin edition of *The Clicking of Cuthbert*. **(CCU–AMT)**

WATTS, Dr Isaac (1674–1748): watched one of his drives from the tee and jotted down on his scorecard:

> Fly, like a youthful hart or roe,
> Over the hills where spices grow.

(HOG–Preface)

WEAKNESS and HUMILITY: the strange sensation which a cave woman might have felt when, with her back against a cliff and unable to dodge, she watched her suitor take his club in the interlocking grip, and, after a preliminary waggle, start his backswing. **(CCU–ROS)**

WELLS, Herbert George (1866–1946): a tense, independent, self–sufficing life seems bleak, like the sort of nightmare suffered after cold pork by,. **(DOS)**

Ramsden Waters explains his point of view to Wilberforce Bray

WEMBLEY, Clarice: one of a trio loved by a twelve–handicapper, née Wembly in **Strand–WIH**. (**MLF–WIH**)

WESTMINSTER KENNEL SHOW: a mongrel rash enough to wander into, would have experienced emotions comparable to those of playing golf in front of hardened experts with caterpillars parading up and down the spinal cord. (**Argosy–BSH; SatEvePost–BSH**)

WESTON, Betty: one of the bright galaxy of golden lads and girls known to the **Oldest Member** from their nursery days. Is one of those ardent and vivid young ladies with a penchant for plumed knights and corsairs of the deep. Having given **Mortimer Sturgis** the brusheroo, she received in return a patent Sturgis, Aluminium, Self–Adjusting, Self–Compensating Putting–Cleek as a symbol of ongoing friendship at the time of her marriage to the charismatic **Eddie Denton**. (**CCU–AMT**)

WIDGEON, Herbert: plays a match in which his opponent is allowed to shout "Boo" three times at self–selected moments. (**CCU–LOH**)

WILCOX, Ella Wheeler (1850–1919): McCay knew her by heart. (**MUP–ARB**)

WILDING: Jack Wilton was described as a W–esque tennis–player. (**MLF–WIH**)

WILLARD, Peter: the outstanding golf cripple. A foozler, a topper, a loser of balls, a wasp–smacker, a Chesney–lighter and sympathiser — in fact a good chap. Holder of the course record at a hundred–and–sixty–one, achieved in his first season. His supporters claim that his drive off the tee entitles him to an unchallenged pre–eminence among the world's most hopeless foozlers. But even he can make light of the last three holes, having occasionally come home in six, five, seven, conceding himself only two eight–foot putts. Despite all this, he believes competition–play to be good for the nerves, perhaps important for one who appears to enjoy marmalade on his breakfast bacon. (**CCU–WOW; HOG–CFO,MPF,PRS; NSE–EXC**)

Lettice Willoughby plotting Rollo's fate

137

WILLIAM: the fictional character regarded as his role model by **Braid Bates**. (NSE–RHR)

WILLIE: to be the proud possessor of a knitted sock. (CCU–WOW)

WILLIS, George: sets the fashion for freak golf matches at **Marvis Bay**. (CCU–LOH)

WILLOUGHBY, Enid: mother of **Lettice**, and sister of **Rollo Podmarsh**, who cheers Rollo up by telling him that they had to poison **Ponto** the other day. (HOG–ARP)

WILLOUGHBY, Lettice: a hearty child, d. of **Rollo Podmarsh**'s sister **Enid**, is a good and persistent trencherman at all times, and particularly rough on the puddings. Believes in making the most of the halcyon childhood years and has no faith in her grandmother's dictum that two helpings of roly–poly lead straight to the family vault. Planned to put Rollo out of his misery as he was very old and wretched, and wanted to use the decease of **Ponto** as a model. But the chemist wouldn't sell her any poison. (HOG–ARP)

WILTON, Jack: one of those men instinctively labelled as "strong", healthy, fit and confident. Six foot high, a combination of Hermes and Apollo, handicap plus two, also plays tennis and the banjo. Told the tale to **Spencer Clay** to avoid having his holiday spoiled, to the consternation of **Mary Campbell**. (MLF–WIH)

WIMPLE, Clifford: all Nature smiled: the air was soft and balmy; and young **Clifford Wimple**, in a new suit of plus fours, had just sunk two balls in the lake and was about to sink a third. And a fourth. (HOG–PRS)

WINDSOR, Duke of (King Edward VIII) (1894–1972): **Cora Spottsworth** once danced with. (NSE–FOC)

WINDY WASTE: a course where **Cyril Delancey** disputed whether he was out of bounds. (HOG–PRS)

WINKLETHORPE, Mr: tells **Eunice Bray** that she is very good with the brassie. Mr Winklethorpe is a great kidder. **(CCU–ROS)**

WISSAHICKY GLEN: home course of the young **Oldest Member**, and scene of **Vincent Jopp**'s spectacular progress to scratch. **(CCU–HEA)**

WITHERBY, Vera: is wooed and won by a lover who uses the interlocking grip. **(NSE–EXC)**

WODEHOUSE, Pelham Grenville (1881–1975): considered "not bad" by **Vladimir Brusiloff**. Not good, but not bad. As a golfer, he was both observant (see **Sound View Golf Club**) and keen on the game (during a golfing tour of Scotland with Ian Hay, he played both Gleneagles and St Andrews), but his prowess was limited. A long hitter, the complementary need for navigational accuracy rather let him down, as witnessed by E Phillips Oppenheim when playing with him at Woking in the 1930s. Appears as author of **Wodehouse on the Niblick**, over his revered copy of which the **Oldest Member** dozes. **(CCU–COC; HOG–JGO)**

WOMAN: the unfathomable, incalculable mystery, the problem men can never hope to solve. **(HOG–RFQ)**

To **Peter Willard** and **James Todd**, the Serpent in the Links of Eden. **(CCU–WOW)**

WOMAN'S SPHERE: magazine to which **James Todd**'s aunt contributed occasional stories. **(CCU–WOW)**

WOODFIELD: the Long Hole village with a garage from which a car emerged, into which **Arthur Jukes** chipped his seven hundred and twelfth using a niblick. **(CCU–LOH)**

WOODHAVEN: where both **Peter Willard** and **James Todd** reside. **(CCU–WOW)**

WOOD HILLS: suburban paradise in which **Mrs Willoughby Smethurst** successfully enacts the part of the serpent by literally introducing poets and other strangers into society. **(CCU–COC)**

WOOLLAM CHERSEY; a big place in Hampshire, inhabited by **Bill Paradene/Bannister, Sir Hugo Drake** and a thousand pigs, which appear to be of a strange breed, as they have to be milked, and the milk is turned into butter using a Holstein Butter–Churner. Parts of the estate date back to the thirteenth century, and there is an oak tree planted by King Charles I. **(DOS; GOO)**

WOOSLEY, Freddie: drops a weak mashie shot into the lake. **(CCU– WOW)**

WOOSTER, Bertram Wilberforce: a sixteen–handicap golfer who always entered the Drones Club Golf tournament, though without conspicuous success. At **Bingley–on–Sea**, for example, he was beaten in the first round

> "And, to increase the mortification of defeat, Jeeves, by a blighter who had not spared himself at the luncheon table and was quite noticeably sozzled."

Evidently, as Jeeves pointed out, he had omitted to keep his eye on the ball with sufficient assiduity. **(VGJ–JKC)**

WORMWOOD SCRUBS: the perceived residence of **Rodney Spelvin's** soul for seven years and the place where bad golfers visit so frequently it is hardly worth while their having their hair cut during their brief intervals of liberty. **(NSE–RHR)**

WORPLE, Rupert: takes a post–graduate course with **Bradbury Fisher** at **Sing–Sing** as student number 8,097,565. **(HOG–KIW)**

WOVEN TEXTILES: being cornered. **(CCU–HEA)**

WRECKING CREW: four retired businessmen, known as **Consul the Almost Human, First Grave–Digger, Man With the Hoe,** and **Old Father Time,** who had taken up the noble game late in life because their doctors had ordered them air and exercise. All respectable men, highly thought of in their respective businesses, but considered in golfing circles to be direct descendants of the **Gadarene Swine.** As they leave a tee, they move with their caddies in mass formation looking like a great race–migration of the Middle Ages. **(HOG–CFO)**

WYNDHAM, Mrs: hostess to **Rodney Spelvin** during his first visit. **(HOG–RFQ)**

X: the unforeseen, the Unknown Factor which pops up and throws a plan of campaign out of gear. **(HOG–RFQ)**

YALE: opposition for **Sing Sing** at the opening of the **Osborne Stadium.** **(HOG–KIW)**

ZAMBESI: filled with sacred crocodiles. **(LEO–ALG)**

ZOROASTER: where in the name of, is our mesh–knit underwear? **(CCU–COG)**

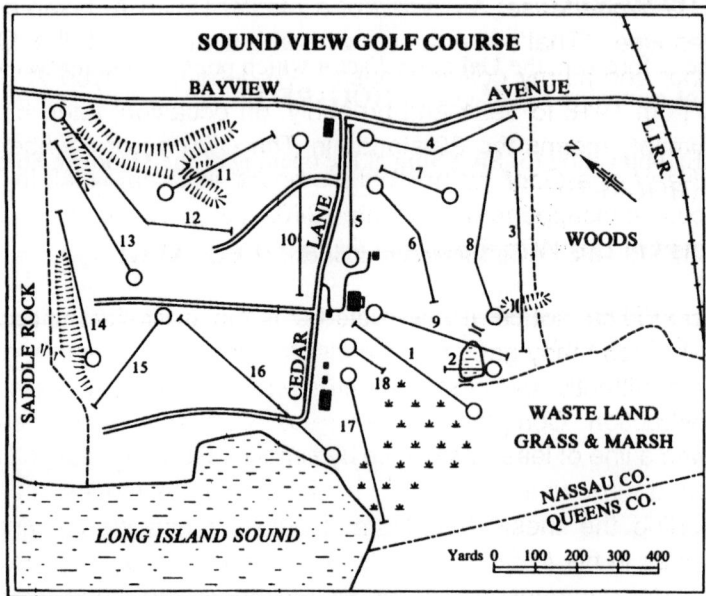

SOUND VIEW GOLF COURSE

BAYVIEW   AVENUE

L.I.R.R.

N

4

11

7

12

5   6   WOODS

10 LANE   8   3

13

SADDLE ROCK

14

15   16

CEDAR

9

1

2

18

17

WASTE LAND
GRASS & MARSH

NASSAU CO.
QUEENS CO.

LONG ISLAND SOUND

Yards 0   100   200   300   400

THE OLDEST MEMBER'S HOME COURSE

An Essay by the late Walter S White

Though disguised by so many aliases and transatlantic crossings, the Oldest Member's home course had a real existence at the Sound View Golf Club in Great Neck, Long Island, New York. In his *P G Wodehouse: A Portrait of a Master* David A Jasen quotes Wodehouse, "That's the place where I wrote about the Oldest Member and all my golfing stories." Wodehouse played at Sound View from 1918 to 1921 and probably, on occasion, later, but "all" presumably means the 20 stories in *The Clicking of Cuthbert* and *The Heart of a Goof*, as he sold his house in Great Neck in 1921. The course disappeared in the late 1940s, taken over by developers, as noted in *Life With Freddie* in *Plum Pie*.

The course cannot be reconstructed from the stories alone because there are too many gaps and inconsistencies. But a search carried on, intermittently, over many months provided the tools for such a reconstruction. Completed, it shows the extent to which Wodehouse followed a line of least resistance by simply describing real golf holes at Sound View when he needed backdrops for his stories, thus fully supporting the thesis that Norman Murphy has so convincingly presented in his *In Search of Blandings*. Furthermore, by providing a basis for comparison, this reconstruction also lets one recognize Wodehouse's stagecraft when he invents a variation to suit a plot or enhance the drama of some action.

The clubhouse and boundaries of part of the course are shown on two old maps reprinted in a 1975 pamphlet entitled *This Is Great Neck*, which also contains a photograph of the clubhouse, unfortunately the side opposite from the Oldest Member's terrace.

143

The topography and cultural features of the area are shown on the US Geological Survey map (2,000 ft/inch) of the Sea Cliff quadrangle. A Long Island collector of golf memorabilia kindly gave me a photocopy of a pre-1931 scorecard. (The name of the course was changed in 1931.) It lists the yardages for all the holes. Finally I was fortunate in locating Joseph DeMane, who had caddied and played at Sound View from 1929 to 1942. His enthusiasm in sharing his detailed recollections of the course has been a delight as well as a tremendous help.

The account presented here has a map compiled by fitting holes of the lengths given by the score card to the topographical and cultural features of the area, using the general layout and supplementary descriptions provided by Joseph DeMane. Before I had the latter in hand I had only been able to plot five holes correctly using the stories alone. As it turns out, the layout and hole lengths are such that one has very little leeway to vary the placement of the holes, so the map should be more than adequate for literary research.

The capsule descriptions of the holes include distances and pars from the score card, lay of the land from the topographic map, and special features of the holes from Joseph DeMane.

Brief descriptions of the holes at Sound View Golf Course:

No 1   355 yds, par 4. Down hill to island green in marsh. (This island green does not figure in any of the stories, and it may represent a post-Wodehouse lengthening of the hole.)

No 2   130 yds, par 3. The Lake Hole needs no introduction.

No 3   485 yds, par 5. Up hill, blind second shot over brow. Gully 50-100 yards from tee, crossed by footbridge.

No 4   385 yds, par 4. Dogleg right, following curve of Bayview Avenue. Bunkers across fairway near bend.

No 5   310 yds, par 4.

No 6   Also 310 yds, par 4. Dogleg left around trees. Drive downhill, then up to elevated green. No bunker on left at bend.

No 7   175 yds, par 3.

No 8   415 yds, par 4. Down hill, then up. No traps.

No 9   338 yds, par 4. Drive over pond, then up hill to elevated green just below clubhouse terrace. Footbridge on path around pond.

No 10   367 yds, par 4. Up over brow of hill.

No 11   307 yds, par 4. Gully across fairway near a green that has bunkers to right and front.

No 12   525 yds, par 5. Dogleg right, gully in front of green.

No 13   356 yds, par 4. Up hill, blind second shot. Bunkers across fairway.

No 14   376 yds, par 4. Down hill. Fairway sloped to right into gully.

No 15   277 yds, par 4. Up hill to elevated green.

No 16   490 yds, par 5. Slight downhill. Dropoff to bay, right of green.

No 17   344 yds, par 4. Drive over marsh, then up hill.

No 18   105 yds, par 3. Straight up hill. Very undulating green.
         Trap across front, another behind.

The order of the holes in the 1930s, when Joseph DeMane played, is the same as that on the score card, but the first and second nines are interchanged compared with their order in almost all the golf stories (early 1920s). The second hole of the stories, the celebrated Lake Hole, is the 11th hole of the 1930s, and so forth. I have numbered the holes so that they show the sequence of the stories (Order A) rather than the sequence as it was in the 1930s (Order B).

On at least four occasions, the Oldest Member refers to changes made between the time a story took place and the time of his narration, but these asides are not consistent with one another and appear to be mere corroborative detail. Only in *Excelsior* (1948 — dates after titles are of the first magazine publication as given in Jasen's *Portrait*) does the interchange of the 9th and 18th holes follow the sequence of Order A to Order B. In *The Magic Plus Fours* (1922), *There's Always Golf* (1936) and *Rodney Has a Relapse* (1949) the change is in the opposite direction, from Order B to Order A. Wodehouse may well have been aware of the change in the mid or late 1920s, but though he did use the later sequence, Order B, in some of the later stories (*Scratch Man* (1940); *Tangled Hearts* (1948)) he used the earlier sequence in others (The *Letter Of The Law* (1936)) as well as *There's Always Golf* and *Rodney Has A Relapse*, just mentioned.

Individuals familiar with the golf stories will find many old friends here: the immortal short second; the Lake Hole (the lake can be visited today in Pond Park, a small private park); the long third up over the brow of the hill; the dogleg fourth and twelfth (the former with its bunkers across the fairway); the fourteenth, the Ravine Hole. One can easily follow the unscrupulous Bingham's shot from the first

146

tee to the 17th fairway en route to his boat by the 16th green as he sets out on *The Long Hole*. The waste land beyond the first green, traversed by Jukes, is still there. (The rest of their route to Times Square can be followed just as easily as all the place names in the US version of the story, unlike those in the UK version, are real and come in proper sequence.) Ravines (gullies) that spell disaster in so many of the stories are all present and accounted for, as are the footbridges, though the only place where a bridge remains today is over the outlet of the lake, where Harold Pickering dunked Sidney McMurdo in *Scratch Man*.

More interesting, in some ways, than the features which Wodehouse described faithfully from originals in their proper places at Sound View, are others that he changed for the purposes of some of the stories, changes that can now be identified. This scene–shifting occurs most commonly at the hole where the story ends. *The Magic Plus Fours*, *Scratch Man* and *Tangled Hearts* all end at the lake, moved to the second nine to make room for nine or more holes before the climax. (Wodehouse obtained the same result in *Rough Stuff* without altering the course by having the round start at the tenth hole.) Where the plot calls for an eighteenth fairway long enough for some mayhem (*Chester Forgets Himself* and *There's Always Golf*) or a slosh at the tee much too powerful to be appropriate for a short par–3 (*Farewell To Legs*), the 18th becomes a par–4. In *Rodney Fails To Qualify*, Wodehouse keeps the essential features of the par–3 seventh, but sets the stage for his watery finish by piping in a river to surround the green. Another invented prop is the Sahara–like bunker on the left of the fairway around the bend of the sixth hole, where the Oldest Member suggested William Bates might propose to Jane. Norman Murphy speculates that Wodehouse's inspiration for this bunker may have been an enormous one that is on the sixth hole at Addington, where Wodehouse datelined his preface to *The Heart Of A Goof*; like the sixth at Sound View, it is a dogleg left, though the bunker is on the right.

Some features that do not fit Sound View do not appear to have been altered to satisfy the needs of a plot or action. Two concrete examples from stories clearly based, overall, on Sound View may be mentioned. *Chester Forgets Himself* (1923) contains the only complete hole–by–hole log for 18 holes. (*Ordeal By Golf* (1919), which describes eleven holes, all of which fit Sound View, is a close second in completeness.) All but the last three holes of *Chester* fit the pre–1931 score card. In the story these have pars of 4, 3 and 4 respectively and par for the course is 71. On the score card pars for these holes are 5, 4 and 3, and par for the course is 72. The 17th hole as shown on the map is so perfectly placed for Bingham's Drive in *The Long Hole* (1921) that the 1930s position is almost certainly correct for Wodehouse's day as well. As suggested earlier, the climax of *Chester* requires a par–4 18th hole, so it looks as though Wodehouse simply interchanged the pars on the last two holes without worrying about their placement. This does not explain why the par–5 16th of the card is a par–4 in the story. Possibly the hole really was lengthened sometime in the late 1920s but, if not, there is no ready explanation for a shortening; the length does not affect the plot.

The Letter Of The Law provides a second example of enigmatic departure from the Sound View model. Five of the eight holes described in the story fit Sound View, but three do not: the 12th hole of the story is a par–4 (drive plus mashie shot), the 376–yard 14th is called 'short' and the 277–yard 15th is twice called 'long'. Perhaps by 1936 some of the details of the course were fading in Wodehouse's mind and he was simply improvising; the intangibleness of 'short' and 'long' rather supports this interpretation.

Of the 31 stories in *The Golf Omnibus* six say nothing about individual golf holes. In 18 stories the golf holes that are depicted generally fit the Sound View course, though the quality of the fit varies from story to story. All eleven holes described in *Ordeal By Golf* fit, as do 15 of the 18 in *Chester Forgets Himself* whereas in three, *Keeping In With Vosper, Scratch Man* and *Tangled Hearts*, the only tie is the Lake Hole. The seven remaining stories do not fit Sound View: *Sundered Hearts, The Clicking Of Cuthbert, The Heel Of Achilles, High Stakes, Farewell To Legs, Feet Of Clay* and *Sleepy Time*. In most of these only one or two holes are mentioned, not enough even to suggest, much less pinpoint, some other course. *High Stakes* (1925) touches on six holes and, with a bit of stretching, the specifications could fit the East Course of the Maidstone Club at East Hampton, Long Island, where Wodehouse summered in 1923. Whether or not the remaining stories have wholly fanciful settings would be difficult to prove, considering the number of courses Wodehouse must have played in the wanderings of his golfing years. Perhaps the sharp dropoff, after 1927, in both the frequency of the golf stories and the Oldest Member's attention to detail occurred because the Sound View Course lost its immediacy as it receded from Wodehouse's present into his past.

This essay is reprinted with the kind consent of Mrs Jean White, widow of the late Walter White, who was himself an eminent Wodehouse collector and scholar.

It first appeared in In Search of Blandings *by N T P Murphy (Secker & Warburg, 1986).*

A Comprehensive Golf Library

Anon	*Grey Eyes That Gleam*	CCU–ROS
	The Badminton Book	CCU–WOW
	The Man of Chilled Steel	CCU–ROS
	The Man with the Missing Eyeball	HOG–JGO
	Gone With The Wind *	FQO–SCM
Auden, Wystan Hugh		NSE–TAH
Bartlett	*Familiar Quotations*	MUP–ARB
Botts, Lavender	*Elves in the Sunshine* (in preparation)	FQO–JBW
	Elves on the Golf Course (possible alt. title)	FQO–JBW
	How To Talk To The Flowers	NSE–EXC, FQO–JBW
	Many of My Best Friends Are Fieldmice	FQO–JBW
	Many of My Best Friends Are Mosquitoes	NSE–EXC
	My Chums The Pixies	NSE–EXC
Braid, James	*Advanced Golf* **	HOG–HST, GOO, DOS, CCU–WOW

*   Unless Harold Pickering is as ill-informed as Ivor Llewellyn in *The Luck of the Bodkins* concerning authors and their works, this will be the one by Margaret Mitchell.

**   As serialised in *C B Fry's Magazine of Action and Outdoor Life*, vol 6, from December 1906.

Braid, James (cont)	*Braid on Taking Turf*	HOG–PRS, GOO, DOS
	On the Pivot	CCU–ROS
	Braid on the Push–Shot	CCU–SGM
	Golf Without Tears	HOG–THG
Brusiloff, Vladimir		CCU–COC
Dell, Ethel M		HOG–PRS
Duncan, George	*On the Divot*	CCU–ROS
Farmer, Prof Pepperidge	*Sleepy Time* ***	PLP–SLT
Flack, Agnes	Unspecified Novel	PLP–SLT
Gibbon, Edward	*Decline and Fall of the Roman Empire*	FQO–SCM
Gooch, John	*Madeline Monk, Murderess Saved From The Scaffold* (in preparation)	MSS–PTT MSS–PTT
	The Mystery of the Severed Ear (in mind)	MSS–PTT
Hagen, Walter	*On Casual Water*	SatEvePost–PRS
Henley, W E		HOG–ARP
MacBean, Sandy	*How to Become a Scratch Man from Your First Season by Studying Photographs*	CCU–WOW

*** (or, *Hypnotism As A Device To Uncover The Unconscious Drives and Mechanism In An Effort To Analyze The Functions Involved Which Give Rise To Emotional Conflicts In The Waking State*)

McBean, Sandy	Same title	CCU–ROS

Marcus Aurelius	*Meditations*	CCU–OBG
Morrison, Alex		NSE–TAH
Nastikoff		CCU–COC
Phipps, Luella Periton	*The Love that Scorches*	HOG–RFQ
Poe, Edgar Allan	*Fall of the House of Usher*	CCU–SUH
	Hints on Golf	MUP–ARB
Proust, Marcel		Cosmo–IGY
Ray, Ted	*On Taking Turf*	CCU–SGM
Rockett, John	*Reminiscences*	FQO–SCM
Rollitt, Dwight Z	*Are You Your Own Master?*	Colliers–OBG
Rollitt, Prof Orlando	*Are You Your Own Master?*	CCU–OBG
Royce, Wilmot	*Grey Mildew*	HOG–CFO
	Sewers of the Soul	HOG–CFO
	The Stench of Life	HOG–CFO
Socrates		FQO–JBW
Sovietski		CCU–COC
Spelvin, Rodney	*The Purple Fan*	HOG–JGO
Spottsworth, Cora McGuffy	*Furnace of Sin*	NSE–FOC
Taylor, John Henry	*Taylor on the Push Shot*	Colliers–OBG
	On the Chip Shot	CCU–ROS

Tolstoy		CCU–COC
Vardon, Harry	*Vardon on the Push Shot*	CCU–COC
	On the Swing	CCU–ROS
	Vardon on Casual Water	HOG–ARP
	What Every Young Golfer Should Know	HOG–RFQ
Wodehouse, P G	*Wodehouse on the Niblick*	HOG–JGO
		CCU–COC